ROYAL REBEL

ALFHEIM ACADEMY: BOOK THREE

S.T. BENDE

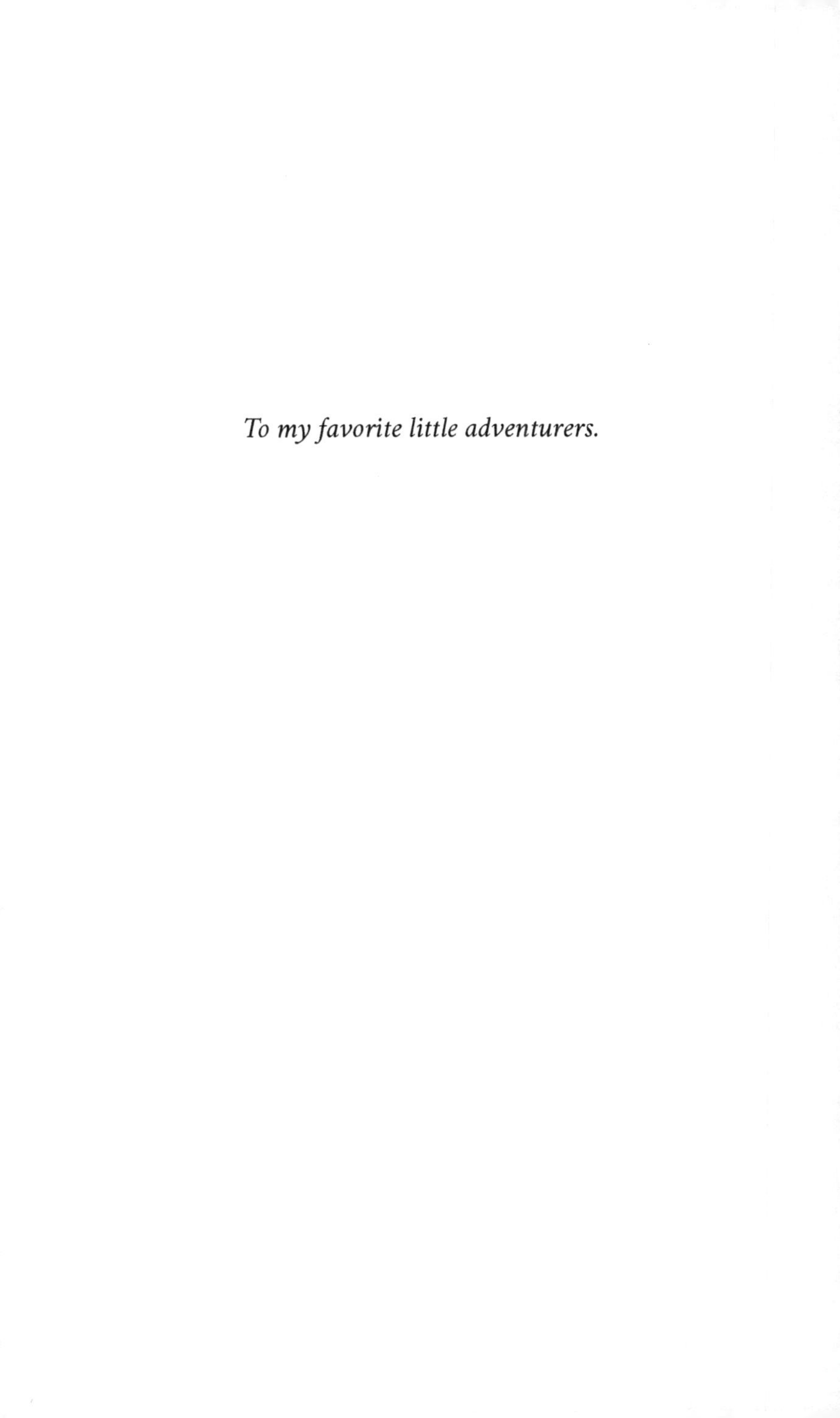

To my favorite little adventurers.

ALSO BY S.T. BENDE

Meet the Vikings in VIKING ACADEMY.

VIKING ACADEMY

VIKING CONSPIRACY

VIKING VOW

Meet the faeries in ALFHEIM ACADEMY:

ALFHEIM ACADEMY

DARK FAERIE

ROYAL REBEL

Meet the Norse God of War in THE ÆRE SAGA:

PERFEKT ORDER

PERFEKT CONTROL

PERFEKT BALANCE

PERFEKT MATCH

Meet the Norse God of Winter in THE ELSKER SAGA:

ELSKER - ENDRE - TRO

Meet the demigods in NIGHT WAR SAGA:

PROTECTOR - DEFENDER - REDEEMER

Complete list of S.T.'s Star Wars children's titles

at http://www.stbende.com/star-wars

"**S**ORRY I'M LATE! MY drills got held up by this bat-*skit* crazy deer who should *not* have wandered onto the *Verge* lawn. Signy thought it might have been a Svartalfheim tracker, so she put the whole class on lockdown, and, well . . ." I dropped into the gilded chair that rested regally beside my grandmother's desk. I raked my fingers through my ponytail, which had tangled considerably on my run to the royal residence. I was *so* not making a good impression. "Anyway, I know you always say that there's no excuse for tardiness. I'm sorry."

"You are forgiven," Constance said primly. She opened a drawer and removed a tissue, which she slid discreetly across her desktop.

"Oh, my nose isn't running," I assured her.

"Perhaps not. But your mascara is." Queen Constance arched one perfectly groomed brow. "And royalty *always* looks their best."

Right.

I took the offered tissue and dabbed at the corners of my eyes. When I'd finished, I pulled my data pad from my bag, leaned back in my chair, and crossed my legs. "So, what's on today's agenda?"

Constance frowned. "Posture."

Double right.

With a sigh, I set my pad on the desk and sat up straight. "Better?"

"It could not have gotten worse," Constance said under her breath.

A smile tugged at my lips. "Is that sarcasm? Am I rubbing off on you after all?"

"Posh." Constance waved her hand. But her eyes sparkled just a bit more, and I knew she appreciated the newfound ease we shared every bit as much as I did.

It had been a long road.

My relationship with Alfheim's ruler had come a long way since our early days of mutual loathing. In the year and a half since I'd forced her to job share, we'd learned to co-exist as regents. We even had a standing weekly tea date, during which she shared pearls of queenly wisdom while I tried not to embarrass myself in front of her ever-present—and ever-judging—staff. But no matter how much time we spent together, I'd never get used to her insane standards of physical perfection. Constance's office was always perfectly kept, her clothing neatly pressed, and I'd never seen so much as a hair out of place from her tightly wound chignon. Me, on the other hand . . . I just wanted to do the job.

Preferably, in combat boots.

"Good. Our tea has *finally* arrived. You may enter." Constance waved at the page hovering in the doorway. The girl glided into the room with the grace characteristic of my grandmother's staff—I secretly suspected that her hiring pool consisted solely of principal dancers from the Royal Alfheim Ballet. The girl set down two china teacups and saucers, then placed a teapot beside each. I knew my grandmother's pot would contain her favorite jasmine tea, while mine, *gods willing*, held my own favorite beverage—

"Hot chocolate for you, Your Majesty." The girl bowed to me.

"Thank you. But again, call me Aura. Your Majesty is my grandmother." I'd told the pages a thousand times I wasn't that into formalities. This girl was new, so I'd give her a pass.

"She will address you by your title." Constance's prim voice cut through the room. "Traditions exist for a reason."

"Progress exists for a reason, too," I muttered under my breath.

"And for you, Your Majesty." The page bowed again, this time to my grandmother. "Your tea was steeped for exactly four minutes, just as you like it."

"Thank you. You may take your leave." Constance waved one hand, then turned her attention back to me. "Where were we? Ah, yes. Today's agenda is brief. It concerns a matter of inter-realm diplomacy, and the merging of our cabinets. Regarding the latter, our official first meeting and swearing in is this evening, and I want to ensure your representatives are prepared."

I smiled at the page as she scurried from Constance's office. "Oh, they're ready. Viggo, Elin, Jande and Finna are excited to settle into the trenches and get things done."

"Governance is an involved process," Constance cautioned. "One steeped in protocols and traditions. I worry that your new appointees aren't sufficiently experienced to handle the tasks that will be put to them."

"My friends will be fine. Elin's going to rock the minister of arts post we created—nobody inspires greatness like she does. Finna and Jande have been working together all their lives, and I know they're excited to bring new ideas as co-ministers of science. And Viggo's more than ready to serve alongside your current minister of defense. He's got plenty of ideas on how to increase our security, while still allowing me to do the job I've trained for as a *Verge*."

"Of course." Doubt clouded Constance's tone. Although she knew my friends had undergone rigorous training over the past few weeks, somehow managing to balance their final semester at Alfheim Academy with a crash course in governance, she still had her doubts about allowing not-quite graduates to fill such important roles.

But my friends were as suited to these roles as cake

was to birthdays. They were each determined to make a difference—the most important job qualification as far as I was concerned.

"Our new ministers have already submitted their policy proposals to Minister Andriskog, and she's approved them all," I reminded Constance. "She's eager to see the changes they'll bring to our joint administration."

Ella Andriskog had taken over Fyrs Narrik's minister of state job when he'd disappeared last year. She'd proven herself adept at navigating the power shift as Narrik's appointees removed themselves from governance, and managed to incorporate both Constance's and my occasionally clashing ideals for a new united Alfheim.

"Yes, well." Constance's lips formed a thin line. "Let our newest ministers not forget that this realm has thrived for thousands of years, in no small part because of its adherence to tradition."

"Tradition's good," I said cautiously. "But change is good, too. Especially with everything that's happened with Narrik, and you, and . . . are you feeling all right?"

Constance removed the back of her hand from her suddenly pale cheek. "I'm fine," she said too quickly.

"Hey." I reached across the table and placed my hand atop hers. "Nobody blames you for what he did to you. You know that."

"I do not," she said primly.

"Narrik drugged you with *älva* dust for years." I shook my head. "You can't be held accountable for the actions you took when your mind wasn't your own."

"I can and I should." My grandmother raised her chin. "A ruler should *never* allow herself to be compromised. My weakness nearly cost this realm everything."

"But we're rebuilding." I squeezed her hand gently. "We've come a long way in the past year."

"And we've still farther to go." Constance withdrew her hand and picked up a single sheet of paper. "Now, if you can in good conscience assure me your friends are prepared for tonight's swearing in, then we may move on to the diplomacy issue. I just received a correspondence from the Crown Princess of Vanaheim. She's asked that we reach out to her posthaste regarding a security issue in her realm."

My eyes widened. "Is Idris all right?"

"Let's ask her ourselves. Since you're emerging as a ruler, I'll let you take the lead in this conversation." Constance tapped a button on her desk, and a beam of light shot from the center of the table. It flickered for a moment, before taking the form of a familiar face.

"Idris!" I grinned at the crown princess. With her rosy cheeks, dewy skin, and the bounty of braids she always wore, she looked more like a homecoming queen than the skilled diplomat I knew her to be. We'd grown close during the past year, bonding over the weirdness that was being a teenager in a royal role. "I didn't know we were going to get to talk to you today."

"It's rather last minute." Idris' perfectly groomed brows knitted together. "We're experiencing a situation in Vanaheim that I believe may impact both of our realms."

Crêpes. "What is it?"

"Do you remember last year when somebody broke into Vanaheim and tried to bribe members of the royal household?"

I leaned toward the hologram. "The perpetrator appeared as a shadow, and wiped your staff's memories so they had no recollection of being asked to grant him entry. The only reason you learned about it was because someone overheard the conversation, right?"

"Correct." Idris folded her hands together. "After you recovered your senators, and Minister Narrik disappeared, everything went back to normal. Until today."

My grandmother and I exchanged worried looks.

"What happened today?" Constance asked.

"Another specter—that's what we're calling the shadows—appeared on Vanaheim. Two of my ladies-in-waiting were walking the palace gardens. The specter must not have seen Lucinda—he cornered Kalynn in the rose garden, wiped her memory, and demanded she disclose her entry code for the palace. Thankfully, Lucinda ran over from the lavender garden and scared him off."

I frowned. "Did Kalynn tell him anything?"

"No." Idris shook her head. "My staff is fiercely loyal, and they would *never* compromise the safety of our realm."

"Yeah, we thought that too. But there are substances

that can impede free will." I avoided looking at my grandmother. I knew how sensitive she was about Narrik's drugging. "Just in case, you might want to rethink your security protocols. How often do you change the entry codes?"

Idris' lips quirked up. "They're retinal scans, so never."

Fair.

"Let me talk to my ministers," I said. "Finna and Jande are doing their final project on something called a resonance code—I don't really understand the science, but I know it has some kind of security implementation. It might be useful."

"I'd love their insight," Idris said honestly. "Put them in touch with me."

"I will," I promised. "Back to the specter—do you have any leads on who's responsible?"

"None." Idris shook her head. "The surveillance footage reads as a shadow—literally, a shadow hovering in front of Kalynn."

"Is there any audio?" I asked.

"Yes. But the quality is abysmal—the words are completely indistinguishable," Idris said.

"It still might prove useful. Send it over, and I'll forward it to the technology division." I made a note. "And I'll ask linguistics to look at it as well. If it's decipherable, someone there should be able to determine the origin by language or dialect."

"Good." Idris nodded. "The last time this happened was right before you discovered your former minister of state was working with Svartalfheim. I hope there isn't another insurgence rising."

"Gods only knows who Narrik's been in contact with since he disappeared." I shuddered. "Do you need backup? We can send a unit."

"My security team is more than capable," Idris assured me. "But our realms *are* both at risk so long as this specter is out there. If you can spare any investigators, it would be to both of our benefits."

I glanced at my grandmother, whose steely-eyed expression was indecipherable. "Let me talk to Queen Constance, and we'll see what we can do."

"Very well. Stay safe, Alfheim." Idris folded her hands together, and bowed her head.

"Stay safe." I lowered my head. When I looked up again, the hologram was gone.

"Well?" Constance said tightly.

"Well, what?"

"Your political ally has requested your aid. What do you intend to do in order to strengthen the strongest alliance Alfheim currently has?"

"Send her an investigative team. Obviously." I picked up my data pad.

"No!" My grandmother barked. My pad clattered to the table at her uncharacteristic break in decorum. "You will personally go to Vanaheim as soon as your schedule allows, and you will assure the crown princess that you are united in wanting to protect her realm."

"Uh, I kind of have finals next week," I reminded Constance.

"All the more reason to go quickly," she countered. "Your graduation is nearly here, after which you will be full-time co-regent of this realm. We do not have many alliances, and it would behoove both of us for you to prioritize the one we can currently count on."

"Yes, but—"

"But nothing." Constance's spine stiffened. "Your coronation is next month. And at that time, you will need to have the backing of—"

Wait. What?

"Next month!" I blurted. "I thought I had a pass until I turned eighteen!"

"You turn eighteen in September." My grandmother spoke as if I were slightly slow.

"I know. And next month is June!" I didn't know what I thought a few months would buy me. *Maybe some sanity?*

"Coronations have always been held in conjunction with the summer solstice." Constance studied her polished fingernails. "It is the time of maximum alignment between the realms, and therefore provides the most synchronous start to a reign."

"Yes . . ." I hedged. "But I think if we went with the autumnal equinox, then maybe—"

"Your coronation will take place on the third Saturday of next month. Invitations to foreign dignitaries will go out next week, after which time we should be able to better approximate our head count."

Constance made a mark on her paper. "Do you have any special requests?"

"That we bypass the ceremony, and get back to the business of governing," I muttered.

Constance swatted the back of my hand.

"Ow! What was that for?"

"As queen, you will do many things you prefer not to," Constance said. "You do them because you love your realm, and its citizens, and more importantly, because being a ruler means living a life of service. And formally welcoming one's new ruler is an important rite of passage. Accept the hand you've been dealt. And *move on.*"

Jeez.

"If you have no requests, I shall tell Eunice to go forward with the organization of your coronation ball. The dance will follow your anointment, and mark the first formal event of your reign."

"Oh. About that." I rubbed my still-stinging hand. "Jande wants to be involved in the planning. I kind of promised him, since I made him miss last year's Solstice Dance."

"We have discussed the importance of doing things a certain way, Aura." Constance peered down her nose at me. "I have allowed you to insert your friends into our governance, but they are hardly equipped to plan an event this steeped in tradition."

"Uh, agree to disagree." I mirrored Constance's steepled-finger pose. "Because if there's one thing

Jande knows, it's how to throw a truly fabulous event. He's an amazing host. Trust me."

Constance's brows pinched together, but she exhaled slowly and said, "Very well. Tell your friend he may set up a meeting with Eunice. To *co*-chair the ball."

Whew.

"Look at us." I grinned. "Compromising. Working together. We've come a long way, haven't we?"

"I suppose that we have." A hint of a smile danced across Constance's face. "Now I suggest you reach out to Vanaheim again, and let their representatives know you will *personally* be seeing to the security situation. We have much ground to cover in restoring our standing amongst the realms. And you, as I am continually told, are our best chance at a brighter future."

No pressure.

I lifted my teapot and poured a generous serving of hot cocoa into my cup. As the thick, chocolatey goodness slid down my throat, I was grateful for the progress we'd made—albeit slowly—in the past year. Alfheim was improving day by day, our citizens were beginning to regain trust in the government, and so far, Narrik had remained locked in whatever portal he'd jumped through nearly a year ago. The question was . . . what was he up to?

And how long would it be before he returned?

CHAPTER 2

LATER THAT NIGHT, MY heart filled with pride. Viggo, Elin, Finna and Jande raised their right hands in front of the full cabinet, and swore to uphold the virtues of Alfheim.

"To honor its values," they chorused. "To preserve its legacy, and to bring light to all of the realms we are sworn to protect. I will serve my community, my realm, and my queens to the best of my ability, so long as I shall live."

My lips parted in a smile as they lowered their hands, and Ella Andriskog turned to the cabinet. "As minister of state, it is my great pleasure to welcome you to Their Majesties' cabinet. I look forward to many years of dedicated public service at your side."

Elin's grin lit up the entire table. She'd dyed the tips of her hair a vibrant purple to mark the occasion, and as she sat, she leaned over to rap her knuckles against Jande's.

"Let's do this," Jande said. Elin nodded in agreement.

When the meeting ended, I hooked my arm through Elin's, and led her out of the council chambers. "I think this calls for a celebration."

"What did you have in mind?" she asked.

"Dessert," I said solemnly. "Lots and lots of dessert."

"It's ten o'clock." Elin shook her head. "The dining hall's been closed for hours."

"Not for the regent." I waggled my eyebrows. "I've got a little something set up for you guys."

"Well in that case . . ." Elin grabbed my hand and tugged me down the hallway.

I glanced over my shoulder to find Viggo standing in the doorway. "Viggo, get a move on. Dessert waits for no man!"

Viggo turned his head, a bemused grin lighting up his angular features. "Tell that to Jande. He's talking the outgoing science minister's ear off about . . . something involving crystals, I think."

"I'll take care of this," Finna offered. She'd been walking our way, but now headed back into the chamber. She emerged a minute later, Jande's elbow hooked firmly around hers. "I know you're excited, Jande, but you need to let the poor man retire in peace!"

"I was going over important ministerial work," Jande huffed.

"Yes, and that work will still be there in the morning. *After* poor Minister Fredag gets some sleep. He looked exhausted!"

"Is that why you dragged me out of there?" Jande scowled. "So Minister Fredag could *rest*?"

"Yes," Finna said frankly. "Also, Elin wants dessert."

Jande's eyes lit up. "We get dessert?"

"If you get your butt back to the academy before eleven, then yes." I shook my head. "I may be co-queen, but I'm powerless when it comes to curfew."

"You should have said that in the first place." Jande picked up his pace. "What are you all waiting for?"

"You!" Finna rolled her eyes.

"Pshaw." Jande charged down the hallway, and was the first into the waiting carriage. When we were all inside, it ferried us back to the academy where, as promised, a sugary buffet awaited us at a window-side table in the great hall.

"Mmm." Elin moaned as she sank her teeth into an éclair. "These are *so good*."

"You're telling me." Finna helped herself to a second cupcake.

"But the mousse," Jande groaned.

I nudged Viggo with my elbow. "Which one's your favorite?"

"Hard to say." He placed a strawberry tart on my plate before helping himself to its lingonberry counter-part. "But I'm pretty impressed you convinced the cooks to do all of this after-hours. I can't even get them to make me a smoothie before my morning workout."

"That's because you exercise at zero dark thirty—Chef Niko is still asleep." I reached up to tweak one of Viggo's inky, black waves.

"I'm your minister of defense now. Gotta make sure my queen's well protected." Viggo grasped my wrist and brought it to his mouth. His lips brushed the sensitive skin on the bottom of my wrist, and a shiver shot straight up my arm. *Yum.*

"You two need a room? And if so, can I eat that?" Jande pointed to the untouched tarts on our plates.

"Leave them alone." Finna swatted her friend. "They haven't had a moment's peace since we all got appointed."

"And we're not about to have many more." I reluctantly removed my wrist from Viggo's lips, and turned to our friends. "Vanaheim asked us to help them with a security issue. Viggo, you and I are going to have to take a quick trip off-realm to investigate another specter issue."

"Specter?" Viggo's brows furrowed together.

"The shadow that appeared last year—the one that caused all that trouble in their realm? It's back. And Crown Princess Idris thinks it's out for *both* of our realms. We need to head to Vanaheim to try and track down the source, and hopefully, imprison it."

"Isn't Maja coming this week?" Viggo asked. "Think she can help us out?"

Viggo's dark faerie cousin had abilities the rest of us didn't. With her ability to control both light *and* dark energy, she was in a unique position to read intentions and discern potential outcomes. Plus, she was a major badass who got *skit* done.

"I'm sure she can," I confirmed. "We'll head off-realm this weekend—and, Frigga willing, be back with time to study up before finals start. In the meantime, Finna and Jande, Idris wants to talk to you about your resonance . . . thing."

"The resonance code?" Jande tilted his head. "Why?"

"The specter's managed to breach Vanaheim's security," I confided. "They're using a straight retinal scan as a keycode, which is good but not breach-proof. I remember you said the resonance code had potential security implementations. Think it could help Idris?"

"Definitely," Finna confirmed. "It's a significantly more secure system than a simple scan."

"Good. I'll message Idris and tell her you'll be in touch in the morning. She'll probably want you to draft some kind of briefing—if it's too much with your exam prep, I'll tell her—"

"We can handle it," Finna said confidently. "We're your ministers of science now—we're going to do everything we can to help Alfheim's allies. "

"You guys are the best," I said gratefully. "Now, eat up. We're in for a crazy month between work and exams and graduation and my coronation—"

"Your coronation?" Viggo glanced down at me. "I thought that wasn't until September."

"Apparently it's in June," I muttered. "Not that Constance asked what I wanted."

"Can I—"

"Yes, Jande." I raised my hand. "You get to co-chair the coronation ball."

"Yes!" Jande fist-pumped the air.

As my friends turned their attention to their desserts, Viggo leaned over to whisper in my ear. "You okay with all of this?"

"Not really," I said honestly. "But like I said, Constance wasn't exactly asking for opinions."

"I'm sorry this is all coming at you so fast." Viggo's fingertips grazed the back of my hand. "Let me know what you need from me."

"Thanks." I turned my hand upward and laced my fingers through his. "I really appreciate it."

He squeezed my palm lightly, then reached for my plate. "You going to eat that?"

"Hey." I batted his hand away. "Get your own dessert."

With a laugh, Viggo tossed his lingonberry tart into his mouth, then took two more from the platter. We eased into relaxed banter with our friends, enjoying the rare night off from our duties. Soon enough, we'd be buried in work and studies and responsibilities and stress.

Again.

"Well, well, well. Look who finally decided to grace us with her presence." The next day, the nasally voice of the girl I'd learned to loathe—again—assaulted my ears. Britney "Bitch Face" Blomgren had emerged from her coma completely unchanged. When she'd been knocked out in our battle with my dark elf uncle,

Dragen, I'd asked the healers to administer extra doses of light. She'd been horrible before the incident, but I was positive she'd awake a changed girl, with nothing but gratitude for her new lease on life.

Shows what I know.

These days, Britney and her *Styra* friends dedicated their free time to planning our graduation party. And, so far as I could tell, to ensuring these last few days of school were as miserable as possible for everyone outside of their social circle. Most of the time, my friends and I just ignored them. We sat at opposite ends of the dining room, and since none of us were in the *Styra* program, we usually managed to steer clear of the mean girl mafia. But once a week, we all had to sit through the same Keys class. It was supposed to be preparing us for the roles we'd be taking on after graduation, but since Britney sat directly in front of me, all it did was give me a massive headache.

No matter what realm you lived on, high school was Helheim.

"Not that it's any of your business, but I was in a meeting. A *confidential* meeting." I ignored Britney's eye roll as I slid into my seat, and pulled my notebook from my bag. Then, I hastily copied today's lecture topic from the smartboard at the front of the room.

Alfheim: Our future.

Gulp.

Elin reached over from where she'd slid into her own seat across the aisle, and squeezed my shoulder. "Ignore Britney. She's worse than usual today."

"You have a problem with me, *Musa?*" Britney leaned forward.

"None that couldn't be solved by you taking a long walk off a short pier." Elin shrugged.

A low growl ripped from Britney's throat, but before she could hurtle what was sure to be a dim-witted insult, our teacher entered the room. Britney slouched back in her chair with a disappointed frown, and I tried to hide my annoyance.

Two more weeks. Two more weeks until I gradu-ated. Then I'd be rid of Britney once and for all. I could handle anything for two weeks. Couldn't I?

"Welcome, ladies and Viggo." Elin's mom, Larkin, taught our Keys class. She'd been responsible for our Alfheim classes back on Midgard, so I was used to her style. Plus, she didn't tolerate any of Britney's B.S.—a fact that endeared her to me even more. "Let's get right into it today. It's been a year of tremendous upheaval for the realm, and as Keys, Alfheim will look to you to continue to steer us on a steady course. I'd like for you to identify four main areas of change, and examine what you, as Keys, can do to guide the realm in an upward direction. Any ideas?"

Sela raised her hand. "Our ecosystems. They suffered extensively during Minister Narrik's tenure. He stripped resources and drove multiple areas to uninhabitable status."

"Correct." Larkin wrote *environment* on the board. "And what can we do to counteract that?"

One of my *Empati* classmates raised her hand.

"Yes, Vira?"

"The restoration teams have been working for nearly a year with great success," Vira began. "Pairs of *Empati* and *Elementar* have successfully brought three regions back from uninhabitable to endangered, and they're well on their way to restoring them fully. Continual support of these teams, and the departments that run them, will provide consistent, result-oriented impact."

"Nice." Larkin noted *restoration team—support* on the board. "Who can name another area of change? Kyler?"

The crimson-haired girl to my left twirled her pen. "Academy admissions. The short-lived ban on all non-pure-blooded Alfheimians was lifted during the last senate vote. Next year's class will be skewed, but moving forward, our school will continue to train a broad group of future leaders."

"And with the Alfheim barrier lifted, off-worlders have integrated fairly seamlessly," Vira added. "*Empati* evaluate intentions, while welcome teams determine the most advantageous placement for new residents, then help them settle into their lives."

"Excellent." Larkin made her notes on the board. "Two more areas of big change. How about you, Aura? What do you think?"

Britney turned around to stare at me.

"Diplomacy, for sure." I ignored Bitch Face. "We've reinstated relationships that fell dormant during our more, uh, trying years."

"And how can you, as Keys, use those relationships

to continue bettering the realm? Britney, we haven't heard from you yet." Larkin wrote *diplomacy* on the smart board, then walked over to Britney's desk.

"We can continue developing relationships. Obviously." Britney flicked a strand of hair over her shoulder.

"By working with our foreign ministers to identify potential allies, and reaching across borders to implement cultural exchanges." Elin crossed her arms.

"Precisely. Well stated." Larkin scrawled on the board, leaving Britney to transfer her glare from me to my bestie. *Typical.*

"And one more area of change . . . Viggo, what do you think?" Larkin asked.

"Governance." Viggo's lips quirked up in a smile. "The regent, her cabinet, and the balance of power within the senate have all completely shifted over the past twelve months."

"Correct. And how can we best support this change in governance? Sela?"

"By striving to uphold the values of *new* Alfheim as we transition into our posts. Regular check-ins with our aligned cabinet members will keep us abreast of any fast-moving changes, while circling back with the department heads we're assigned to support will ensure implementation of new policies."

"You guys are on fire today." Larkin turned away from the board. "Your ministers and department heads are going to be in very capable hands."

"Excuse me?" Britney tossed her hair. It cascaded

over her shoulder like a glossy waterfall. "I haven't been assigned a minister yet. Or a department head."

"Yes, well." Larkin pressed her lips together. "There seems to be a bit of a . . . setback with your assignment."

Don't laugh, Aura. Do. Not. Laugh.

My hand flew to my face to disguise my smile. Signy had told me all about Britney's 'setback.' It seemed that in spite of her being a Key, and medically cleared to resume both studies and work, none of the ministers wanted her. Apparently, being unapologetically awful did not grant one many job prospects.

Snort.

"I'm sure the matter will be resolved shortly. In the meantime, I want each of you to write an action plan pertaining to your assigned discipline. Explain how your studies here at the academy have prepared you to assist in your unique roles as Keys, and make sure your explanation is pertinent to the cabinet member and department head to whom you'll be reporting. Britney, so that you have a framework for this assignment, you may write as if you were serving under me. Aura, Viggo and Elin, since you hold seats on the cabinet, I want your papers to focus on how your studies have prepared you to best serve the departments that now report to you."

"Got it." Elin jotted a note on her pad.

"You will have thirty minutes to outline, then we'll present to the group. As Keys, your opinions are valued. But your ability to convince others to follow your advice will mean the difference between being able to implement the changes you were born to bring about, and being a mere figurehead."

Like my grandmother had been, for so many years . . .

"Get writing." Larkin walked to her desk, and turned over the bubble-filled hourglass that served as her timer. "May the words be with you."

CHAPTER 3

AS SOON AS CLASS ended, I headed to the *Dyr* facility to visit my bobcat friend, Bob. He'd been living there for a little more than a year—since the blowout with my evil Uncle Dragen, during which he'd nearly died. His recovery had been slow, and at my request, the animal husbandry team had kept him under close watch—a life-saving call I'd have thought Bob would appreciate. Instead, it seemed to have ticked him off. Unlike most Midgardian bobcats, Bob could talk—a side effect of his inter-realm travel, I supposed. And because of that, I knew in excruciating detail just how dull he found his confinement, his caretakers, and, as he called them, his cell mates. He described his weekly furlough into the forest in great detail during our hour-long chat, and dropped some not-so-subtle hints at wanting more hall passes from his "keepers"— Bob's words. It had taken me a full ten minutes of explaining before Bob understood he was *nearly*

healed, and he wouldn't let me leave until I'd sworn to talk to the *Dyr* the moment he passed his final physical. For both of our sakes, I hoped that wouldn't take long.

Dinner was halfway over by the time I made it to the great hall. After eating two helpings of roast and potatoes, and taking an unusually short post-dinner walk with my equally wiped-out boyfriend, I decided to turn in early. I kissed Viggo goodnight at my door, then made a beeline for the layers of downy white goodness nestled atop my four-poster bed. I desperately needed some sleep.

Unfortunately for me, Jande had other plans.

"It needs another evidentiary citation." My friend hovered over Finna's desk, toying with the massive purple crystal he wore on his right hand. He always played with his jewelry when he was stressed. He and Finna had been hard at work on their protection briefing since their call with Idris early that afternoon. From the worry lines stretching across their foreheads, I guessed things weren't going well.

"We already have three cases, Jande. I think we're good." Finna's normally tranquil voice carried a hint of tension. "Let's just turn this over and—"

"No! It's our first briefing, and we're writing it for royalty. It needs to be *perfekt.*" Jande spun the ring around his finger.

"Um, could you back up just a bit please? It's hard to write when you're literally leaning on my shoulder."

"Huh? Right. Sorry." Jande stepped a few inches away from Finna's chair.

My roommate ran her fingertip along her data pad. "How's this? We include one final example—the southern icelands restoration. The team reversed the temperature increase brought on by the mining emissions, stopping the melting trend and preserving the water level before it destroyed the audrugulls' nesting grounds."

Jande leaned forward. "Ooh, that's a good one."

"A little space please," Finna said tersely.

Clearly, it had been a long day for our science team, as well.

"Hey, you guys." I walked cautiously toward the edge of my bed. "Nearly done with that briefing?"

"Why? Did Idris ask? Oh, gods, I *told* you we should have finished it before dinner!"

"Stop it, Jande!" Finna turned around. Her russet skin was tinted pink. "We are doing the best we can!"

"Idris didn't say anything," I said quickly. "And it's fine. Just get your report to her whenever it's done. No worries."

"No worr—do you even hear yourself?" Jande placed his hand on his hip. "The Crown Princess of Vanaheim asked us to prepare a security briefing. Van-a-heim. A realm where actual deities and demigods live. Vanaheim."

"I'm familiar with Vanaheim. Thanks." I kicked my shoes into my closet, and pulled my favorite blue pajamas from my wardrobe.

"Have you been there? Do you have any idea what kind of format they use for their official reports, or whether they prefer more formal language in their communi—"

"Are you planning to follow me into the bathroom?" I paused outside the door, my pajamas in hand. I stepped inside, set them on the counter, and placed my palms on Jande's shoulders. "Breathe, Jande. You and Finna are top of your class. I put you on the cabinet for a reason. I have absolute faith in you both."

"I just don't want to screw this up," he whispered.

"You won't. Now let me put on my pajamas, for the love of Frigga. I'm tired."

I closed the bathroom door behind me, and took my time changing, washing my face, and brushing my teeth. By the time I checked my reflection in the silver-framed mirror, turned off the chandelier, and stepped back into my room, a considerably less-stressed Jande lay spread-eagled on Finna's bed. My roommate stood over her data pad, reading silently.

"Everything all right?" I asked again.

"We sent it." Finna brushed an errant strand of hair from her face. "Just waiting on confirmation . . . ah, there it is."

"Thank gods." Jande exhaled. "That was exhausting."

Finna shot him a look. "You do realize this is the job, right? Producing content on short notice for high-ranking officials?"

"It's *part* of the job," I offered. "Some days, you'll oversee research. Or brainstorm workarounds for issues that plague communities."

"Either way, if you're going to melt down on me

every time we have a deadline, I'm out." Finna crossed her arms.

Jande pushed himself up on his elbows. "I didn't melt down. I came up with two of the four examples we cited."

"And you completely stressed me out while doing it! If you want to work together, you're going to have to take it down a notch."

"I can do that," Jande said calmly. "I'll just wear more amethyst."

"And lepidolite," Finna muttered.

"It wouldn't hurt," Jande agreed.

"Now that that's settled . . ." I climbed into bed, and pulled the plush comforter over my legs. *So close to sleep.* "Mind explaining to me what your solution actually was? We kind of blew right past it during our chat."

"The resonance code?" Jande sat all the way up. "We just learned it this semester. But it's *perfekt* for what Idris needs."

"Explain." I leaned back against my pillows.

"Well," Jande began. "Last term, we started an interdisciplinary project with the fourth-year *Empati* class. We wanted to see if we could combine our abilities to create a unique energy signature. Something that might have security implications, since the government's been going through so much change."

"I'm lost," I admitted.

"Basically, we didn't want to find ourselves in a position where someone could be forced to act against their will again." Finna spoke quietly. I'd confided in my friends about Narrik using *älva* dust to control my grandmother. But they knew that the queen was ashamed she'd been deceived, and so we kept the details between ourselves. "Since crystals carry such a unique energetic vibration, we thought we might be able to match the frequency of one with the frequency of an individual's aura—essentially, find an energetic twin that would lock the resonance of its owner in place."

"Okay," I said slowly. "So, did you find any matches?"

"We did," Finna confirmed.

"And what happened?"

"Something we hadn't anticipated," Jande admitted. "We'd thought that once combined, the matching resonances would lock in on each other—hold their identical vibrations in a continual wave. Instead, when the subject held its paired crystal, that subject's energy combined with the crystal's to create a totally unique vibration. One that couldn't possibly be replicated, because in all of our tests, it had never previously existed."

"Wow."

"You're telling us." Jande ran his fingertip along his quartz necklace. "But what's really interesting is the way that vibration shifts once the aura itself changes. It becomes almost stagnant—as if the crystal's putting off no energy whatsoever."

"Like somebody pressed its pause, or mute button?" I asked.

"Exactly," Finna confirmed.

"And that's interesting . . . why?"

"Because if we can match an uncompromised subject to its twin crystal, and record their merged, *unique* resonance code, then we have a formula for that person's imprint *when they aren't under any undue influence.* The minute you ask them to do something that goes against their core values, their aura shifts to one of unease. When that happens, the crystal's resonance disappears, and you know the subject's integrity—and quite possibly, their free will—has been compromised. From a security perspective, that person would be deemed inadmissible to high-clearance situations. You don't want to risk a traitor being around secure documents, or in confidential meetings, right?"

"Right," I agreed.

"Well, now you'll know *when* someone's under undue influence. So long as they've been crystal matched first." Jande looked inordinately pleased with himself. I had to admit, it sounded like a foolproof plan.

"The resonance code—that unique energy signature produced by an uncompromised subject and his or her matching crystal—is a security system that absolutely cannot be hacked." Finna pushed Jande's feet out of the way, and sat on the edge of her bed. "Look, an eyeball can be removed, right?"

"Ew." I cringed.

"It can," Jande said matter-of-factly. "Or it can be 3-D scanned and printed in duplicate. Vanaheim's current use of a retinal scan is a fallible security system. But the code created when a crystal and an aura align can never be matched. If the royal household were to wear their twin crystals, we could set up scanners that would *only* admit certain resonance codes to the castle, or the senate building, or wherever that realm's restricted areas are."

"But couldn't whoever's trying to break into their castle—that specter/shadow/whoever it is . . . couldn't they force someone to scan themselves in, and just follow after them?" I stuffed a second pillow beneath my head so I could see my friends better.

"Not unless that staff member was *willingly* betraying the crown," Finna said. "The resonance of an aura shifts, depending on its owner's mood, intentions, and overall state of mind. If that staff member is being held under duress, or if their mind is being controlled by, say, *älva* dust, then their aura will shift, too. In that case, it will no longer match the resonance of the crystal. And the entry code won't work."

"That's really smart." I blinked at Finna and Jande. "Why didn't we think of that before?"

"To be honest, we weren't sure it could be done. Nobody's ever tried to lock resonances, though of course now it seems completely obvious, and clearly something we should have implemented years ago." Jande sighed. "Oh, well. We have it now."

"We do." Finna nodded. "And we've shared our technical breakdown with Crown Princess Idris' staff. Hopefully, they'll be able to crack the resonances of their key household members, and track crystals that match that vibration."

"And if not, I would be *happy* to make a trip to Vanaheim to personally oversee the project." Jande waggled his brows. "I hear Tyr goes there sometimes."

"Tyr, as in, Asgard's God of War, Tyr? Don't you already have a boyfriend? My super-awesome cousin, perhaps?" I frowned.

"Oh, Ondyr can come too." Jande smiled beatifically. "The more the merrier."

A massive yawn parted my lips. I covered my mouth before rolling onto my side. "It's too late for this. I have to get some sleep. Maja's coming in the morning."

"She is?" Interest piqued Finna's voice. "How long will she be here?"

"A few weeks, I think. She's coming to shadow Viggo to see where our defensive holes might be."

"Will she be here through your coronation?" Jande asked.

"If they're really making me do it in June, I guess so."

Jande rested his chin on his hand. "I don't know why you're so down on all of this. I'd love to be in your shoes."

"You can have my shoes," I said into my pillow. "I don't want any of the attention. I just want to do the job."

"This *is* the job," Finna said gently. "Just like we have to get used to working under deadline *calmly*—"

"Don't glare at me, Finna," Jande interrupted.

"Just like we have our learning curve, you also have to get used to doing these public things. I know you hate them," Finna said, "but they mean a lot to Alfheim."

"I guess," I muttered.

"Just try to have some fun with it," Finna said. "Who knows? You might end up enjoying yourself."

Fat chance.

THE NEXT DAY, VIGGO and I waited outside the school's main entry. Maja, Viggo's dark faerie cousin, and the girl who'd taught me to balance light and dark energies, would be there any minute. After considerable begging, she'd agreed to join my cabinet as a consultant . . . on a *trial* basis only. I'd told Finna and Jande that she'd be shadowing Viggo in his role as minister of defense, but things were a little more complicated than that. She'd also be working with Signy and the *Protektors* to get a better understanding of the threats our realm faced, and helping us evaluate our current staff to identify who might still be loyal to Narrik. Maja's gifts ranged from reading auras to seeing the future to being a kick-butt energy warrior. She was an asset we desperately needed on our team.

I hoped we could convince her to stay.

"Is that her?" I bounced on my toes as a flash of lightning shot across the grey sky.

"She's not Thor. She doesn't travel by lightning." Viggo rolled his eyes.

"Thor doesn't travel by lightning. He travels by Bifrost." I jutted my hip. "And he's God of Thunder, not Lightning, thank you very much."

"Mmm. You and Thor are on close terms then, I take it?"

I wish.

"Not as of yet." I raised my chin. "But we will be. I'm sure the Queen of Alfheim has many dealings with the God of . . . uh . . ."

"Thunder. You *just* corrected me. Are you—"

I pressed my fingers to Viggo's lips. "Shh. Do you hear that?"

"The boom of distant thunder?" Viggo mumbled around the obstruction. "Yes."

"No. That buzzing. It's coming from . . ." I turned in a slow circle. "From . . . *oof!*"

Wind rushed from my lungs as something knocked into me from the side. I was launched into my boyfriend's back. The two of us landed hard against the dirt. When we stopped skidding, I lifted my head to find the knee-high boots, black tights, and goth-chic minidress of the faerie who'd helped me save our realm.

"Maja?" I extracted myself from atop Viggo's prone body. "Jeez, you know how to make an entrance."

"Some *Verge* you two are. Didn't even see me coming." Maja shook her head.

"We were expecting a more dignified arrival," Viggo said drily. He pushed himself up, and pointed to the grassy field in front of the academy. "Ever heard of a landing area?"

"Ever heard of never letting your guard down? No wonder you guys got yourselves in such a mess." Maja shook her head, her inky black waves a longer version of Viggo's.

"That was my grandmother's mess, not mine. We're doing things differently from here on out." I held out my hand and Maja grasped it.

"Then I suggest you never let your guard down." Maja released my hand, and stepped back to appraise the academy. Her brows arched ever-so slightly. Was Maja actually . . . impressed? "So, this is your school? Some castle."

"It is," I said fondly. "It dates back to my grandparents' reign. They mandated that all youth be given the opportunity to receive a formal education in hopes future generations would feel a sense of ownership over their realm, and know they had the tools to make the changes they deemed most necessary."

"Good goal." Maja's eyes traveled upward. "Who are they?"

I followed her gaze to the *Styra/Astral* tower. Our master manipulators and future predictors stood in their respective classrooms, with their nosy noses pressed to the windows. *Typical.*

"Those are the mean girls," I said. "Their disciplines involve looking to the future and projecting the course of events . . . and trying to convince the rest of us to do what they want us to."

Maja's brow quirked. "And how many of them take advantage of that?"

"A good number." Viggo dusted the dirt off his pants. "Hey, cousin."

"Hey." Maja nodded at Viggo. "So, their divisions are the first we'll investigate for potential leaks."

"Some are petty, but most work toward the greater good," I offered. "A few of them are working with the restoration teams to project which regions will suffer the most without immediate correction."

"Mmm." Maja stared at the windows until the occupants finally disappeared. "I'll keep an eye on them."

"Probably a good idea." Viggo gestured to the main entry. "What do you say? Want to take the tour?"

"Always good to get the lay of the land." Maja walked toward the massive double doors that served as the academy's entrance.

"Don't you have any bags?" I glanced around to see if anything had fallen when Maja had tackled us, but I didn't see so much as a backpack.

"I travel light." Maja patted the satchel she wore around her chest. "Besides, you're the queen. I'm sure your ladies-in-waiting can help if I forgot something."

"I don't have ladies-in-waiting. I'm low-maintenance, remember?"

"Uh-huh," Maja said drily. "I see you're still wearing the necklace I made you."

"You said I might need it again someday." I shrugged. "Figured wearing it was a good idea."

It had been almost a year since Maja had fashioned the necklace from a protection crystal. She'd told me I could use it to control the light and dark energies she'd taught me to blend, then wield as a defense. Like me, Maja was a dark faerie—half Alfheimian, half Svartish—and was uniquely able to balance the dueling energies within herself. Although I'd learned to do the same, I'd never be the master that Maja was. In all likelihood, I'd be using that necklace as a crutch for the rest of my life.

"Well, it suits you."

My breath stilled at Maja's rare compliment.

"It's kicked your aura up a notch—it's considerably less muddied than it was the last time I saw you."

"Um, thanks?"

"What about me, cousin? How shiny is my aura?" Viggo's lips quirked upward.

"Dull as your wit," Maja retorted. "Now, are you going to show me this castle of yours or what?"

"This is just the school," I said as I walked toward the entry. "The 'castle' would be the royal residence. It's about a twenty-minute jog that way."

"I just flew eight hours. I'm not up for a jog."

"I didn't say you were. I was just trying to—"

"I'm kidding, Aura," Maja said. Then under her breath, she muttered, "Kind of."

I never knew where I stood with her.

"How's that friend of yours?" Maja studied her nails. "The guy who fought off the guards in the cave last year?"

"Ondyr? He's my cousin, and he's great." I grinned. "Kicking butt in the training ring, graduating with honors, and, hopefully, coming to work with me and Viggo in some *Verge* capacity—though we're still figuring out what exactly that will be."

"Mmm. And how's the other one who fought in the cave?" Maja asked. "The tall one who took down two guards with one sword?"

"You must mean Zara," I said. "She's great, too. She wants to be a *Protektor* after graduation, and I'm hoping she'll want to come on as one of my personal guards once I'm, well . . ."

"Once you're queen of all Alfheim?" Maja arched her brow.

"Once I'm *officially* co-ruler, yes."

"Can't the queen take care of herself?" Maja asked.

"This one can," Viggo said with a grin. "But protocol dictates she have two full-time guards, just in case. Aura hates the idea of some strangers looking out for her, so she convinced the powers that be to let her choose her own *Protektors*. She's bringing in Professor Bergen, obviously, and she's asked Zara to take the second spot."

"And has Zara accepted?"

"She's thinking about it," I said. "She's an action girl, and I think she's worried guarding me will be less exciting than, say, doing undercover work on Muspel-heim. Which is fair."

"Ondyr's working on her though." Viggo opened the castle door, and gestured for us to head inside. "They're training partners, and they've grown really close during the past year. He's going to be working with us after graduation, and I know he wants her to stick around."

"I always did like my cousin." I grinned.

"So, this is the entrance to your school?" Maja looked around as Viggo closed the door behind us.

"It is. And the great hall's this way." Viggo pointed. "Let's start our tour there. Lunch just ended, but I'm sure they still have plenty of food. You've got to be hungry."

"Starving," Maja confirmed.

"We'll give you the tour after lunch then." Viggo followed us down the hallway. "And we'll fill you in on the latest development with our allies."

"Oh, no. What's happening in Vanaheim?" Maja glanced at the main staircase, where a group of first-year students ogled her openly. To be fair, she was the only one not wearing the regulation uniform.

"How'd you know he was talking about Vanaheim?" I waved the first-years away, and they shifted their focus from Maja back to each other.

"Alfheim only has one ally." Maja's skirt swished as she walked. "Asgard still regards us with caution, Midgard doesn't know we exist, and Nidavellir won't trust us for another two decades."

"Really?" I hung a left at the big bay windows. "So, we will earn the dwarves back, then? How do we do it? We've got a foreign affairs team that can—"

"I thought you didn't want to know your future," Maja said wryly.

"I didn't. I don't. But if it's a matter of solidifying relations between the realms . . ."

Viggo's disapproving look stopped my thought.

"Oh, fine. We'll do it the hard way," I muttered.

"The right way's not always the easiest," he reminded me.

"You stole that from a bumper sticker," I accused.

"What's a bumper sticker?" He cocked his head.

"Midgardian thing." I sighed. "Never mind. We're here, anyway."

I led Maja and Viggo through the ornate doors of the great hall. Most of the tables had been cleared and reset for dinner, but one near the window wall remained empty. We took three of the four seats, giving Maja the best view of the forest that backed up to the school.

"Three place settings, please," I said to nobody. A trio of plates, stemware, and glasses appeared instantaneously, along with a massive bowl of salad.

"What the Helheim?" Maja's eyes widened.

"Telepaths take care of the tables," I explained. "If there's something special you'd like for lunch, let them know and they can send it up."

Maja shook her head. "This place is bizarre."

"You don't know the half of it." I dished a heaping

pile of lettuce, carrots, jicama and croutons onto Maja's salad plate, then did the same for Viggo and myself.

"You don't have servants to do that for you?" Maja quirked her brow. "You're the queen."

"I'm not officially the queen for another month," I corrected. "And I told you, I'm low-maintenance."

"We'll see about that." Maja forked her lettuce and took a bite.

"She's *mostly* low-maintenance." Viggo's eyes sparkled. "She does get pretty demanding in the training ring."

"Only when my partner is being lazy, and needs to be reminded that the safety of our realm is directly proportional to the amount of effort he puts in at the *Verge* center." I speared a carrot.

"Mmm. Who holds the record number of wins in hand-to-hand combat?" Viggo's dimple popped.

"And who holds the record for aerial sequences?" I countered.

"I get it. You're both competitive." Maja set her fork down. "Now what's the situation in Vanaheim?"

Viggo quickly filled her in on the recent security breach.

Maja's eyes narrowed. "Do you think the specter is tied to Narrik?"

"We don't know," Viggo said. "And we don't know why the specter wants into the castle. I'm assuming he's trying to gain access to someone more powerful than the household staff. But to do what, we just aren't sure."

Maja put down her fork. "What are you planning to do about it?"

"We're going to Vanaheim. All three of us," I announced. "Viggo and I have finals next week, so this has to be a quick trip. If we go this weekend, we can be back by Sunday night and home in time for our first test on Tuesday. I hope."

"You hope because you're looking for a quick resolution, or you hope because you have exams?" Maja asked.

"Both."

"Aura. An existential threat faces your realm, and you're worried about your grade-point average?"

Well, when she put it like that . . .

"Regardless, I can work with the time we're given." Maja closed her eyes and went perfectly still. I knew her well enough at this point to realize she was meditating. Or looking into the future. Or doing . . . whatever it was she did.

"We'll leave early Friday morning." Her eyes opened as she made the announcement. "That will give us a full three days. Four, if we need to stay on to question any suspects."

"I doubt the specter stuck around." I blinked as a plate of open-faced sandwiches suddenly appeared atop the table. "Thank you," I again said to no one.

"I'm sure he didn't." Maja lifted a sandwich onto her plate. "But he may have accomplices—plants somewhere within the realm."

Viggo filled his dish. "Idris was pretty sure none of her household staff would betray her."

"Who said we're only interviewing her staff?" Maja asked.

Ooh. Smart.

Maja bit into her food. "Mmm. This is good."

"Everything is," I admitted. "I don't know what I'm going to do when I graduate and have to cook for myself."

"You'll be the queen. I doubt you'll be cooking for yourself," Maja said.

Oh. Right.

"If you came to work with us full-time, you'd have access to the royal dining hall too . . ." I dangled the proverbial carrot.

"I told you I'd think about it. We'll see how things go over the next few weeks." Maja took another bite, then glanced at Viggo. "What are you doing?"

"Getting us Bifrost clearance for Friday," he answered. He finished typing on his wrist communicator, then tucked into his food.

"Are off-realm transports still difficult?" Maja asked.

"Nope. We've worked through all the barrier issues, and now it's just a matter of getting the foreign affairs and the transport ministers to sign off on our—"

A *ping* from Viggo's com interrupted my explanation.

"We're all set." He looked up from his watch. "We'll

leave at seven a.m., and signal for a return transport sometime on Sunday. They'll keep us on their scanner."

"Good. And after lunch, tell me everything you know about Vanaheim's royal family. Friendships, relationships, hobbies, areas of interest—maybe there's something in there that could flag a link." Maja took a drink from her crystal glass. "Are all your place settings this fancy?"

"Yes," Viggo and I said in unison.

I sighed. "Overkill, right?"

Maja just shook her head.

We ate in silence for the next few minutes, filling our stomachs with bread and cheese and meat. When we were done, I set my napkin beside my plate and turned to Maja.

"We'll definitely brief you on Idris and her family. And we'll give you a full tour of the academy." I glanced at my own com, which had a slew of incoming messages. I discreetly flashed the last one at Viggo. "But first, you have some friends who want to catch up with you. Quick stop-over in our common room?"

Maja dabbed her napkin to her lips. "I'm not big on friends."

"Well, we are. And you're here now, so get over it." Viggo stood.

Maja quirked her brow. "My, my, cousin. You're becoming quite the leader."

"Just get up and follow me." Viggo rolled his eyes. "If Jande doesn't get to see you, we'll never hear the end of it."

CHAPTER 5

HEAVY GREY CLOUDS SHADOWED the sky when the three of us touched down in a Vanaheim meadow. The unseasonal weather shift had made entry difficult, and queasiness wracked my stomach as I stumbled out of the Bifrost. It was only my second transport—my first without the barrier in place—and though I knew inter-realm transit wasn't easy under normal circumstances, I had no desire to travel in a storm again. *Ever.*

Maja and Viggo walked out of the rainbow wind tunnel, both looking considerably more in control of themselves than I felt. While I struggled to stand upright, Maja checked the com we'd given her and scanned the area.

"If we head due south, we'll be there in less than five minutes," she announced.

"We're off target. Oh, well. Are we flying or walking?" Viggo rubbed tight circles on the small of my back. "You okay, *Glitre?*"

"Never better," I groaned. "Please say walking. I have zero interest in flying right now."

"Fine. We'll walk." Maja turned her com off, and headed my way. "You'd better suck it up, princess. Gods only knows what we're going to find here, and if it's anything like what I suspect, we're in for one Helheim of a—"

"Aura! What are you doing way out here? Didn't we approve your landing just outside the gardens?"

I turned at the sound of Crown Princess Idris' lyrical voice. She and two men crested the meadow on horseback. The animals loped toward us, their golden manes and tails streaming behind their white fur. It wasn't until they were nearly on top of us that I noticed the matching horn spiraling out of the animals' foreheads.

"Unicorns are *real?*" I blurted.

"Of course they're real." Idris knitted her brows together. In her all-white riding gear and pale blond braids streaked with lavender highlights, she looked like a cross between an angel and a hippie. "Why, do Alfheimians believe they're not?"

"I—uh—I . . ." I had no idea. But for a girl who'd grown up on Midgard, this was a *massive* mind blow.

"We are aware of unicorns." Maja looked at me like I was a complete idiot.

"Yeah, well, the dark elves aren't. I never heard of

horned horses when I lived on Svartalfheim." Viggo reached out with one hand. "Can I touch it?"

"Bow first," Idris warned.

"Oh. Right." Viggo flushed. "Apologies, Crown Princess. I—"

"Not to me. To my unicorn." Idris laughed. "She's very protective of me, and if she thinks you're a threat she'll gore you with her horn."

Note to self: stay on unicorns' good sides.

"Of course." Viggo folded his hands together and bowed, hinging at the hip. When he rose, Idris' violet eyes twinkled.

"You should be good now," she confirmed.

Viggo stepped closer to the animal, and offered his hand. The unicorn sniffed delicately, then lowered her head for my boyfriend to pat. Her two unicorn friends tilted their heads in seeming curiosity.

This is insane.

"That's it. I'm bowing too. Can I pat any of them, or is yours the alpha?" I had no idea how unicorn hierarchy worked.

"She is," Idris confirmed. "Start with Sparkles—once she knows you, you can move on to the others without the formalities."

"You named an animal Sparkles?" Maja's disdain was evident.

"Of course." Idris stroked Sparkles' mane. "What do you name your animals?"

I flashed back to the behemoth elephant-sheep that

populated Maja's homeland. My hand flew to my mouth, but my snort escaped nonetheless.

"Sorry," I mumbled through my laughter. "You two just come from *really* different worlds."

"That's fair." Idris crinkled her eyes. "Do you want to pat Sparkles or not?"

"Oh, definitely yes." I bowed deeply. "May I please pat you, oh most beautiful Sparkles? I've never seen a real unicorn before, and—"

"She said bow," Maja reminded me. "Not talk."

I righted myself and reached out with one hand. "Maja, I have seriously got to get you to appreciate the small stuff. Or the big stuff—seeing a real unicorn is— oh my gods, she is so soft!"

"She is." Idris beamed. "They all are. Go ahead. See for yourself."

I glanced up at the stone-faced man sitting atop one of the creatures. "Is it okay with you, or—"

"Hans doesn't speak," Idris offered. "None of them do. But Blossom won't mind, will you, beautiful?"

"Got it." I transferred my attention from Sparkles to Blossom. "I take it these are your newest guards?"

"Yep." Idris sounded resigned. Her parents were the overprotective type, and they'd saddled her with sets of indistinguishable guards for as long as I'd known her. For security purposes, they insisted on switching the teams out every few weeks.

"Ah. Well, it's a pleasure to meet you Hans and, uh . . ." I stared at the second guard, but he remained silent.

"I'm going with Hans and Jans for this team." Idris shrugged.

"Fair enough. Good to meet you both." I offered a cheery smile.

Jans glowered back at me.

Gulp.

"I like him," Maja announced.

"You would," Viggo said. "What's the third unicorn's name?"

"Barry." Idris didn't bat an eye.

"Barry?" I stared at my friend. "Their names are Sparkles, Blossom, and *Barry*?"

"I named him after my favorite uncle—Barrylius."

"Okay." I choked back my laugh. "Great to meet you Barr—ooh, he's even softer than Blossom! Jeez, what do these things eat?"

"Organic hay, four-leaf clovers, and daffodils. But I think it's the rainbow dust supplements that really give them their shine." Idris stroked Sparkles' mane fondly.

"Rainbow dust? What is that?" Viggo asked.

"Dust. From a rainbow." Maja crossed her arms. "Are you even listening?"

"I know we're family, but I swear to Frigga, Maja, if you don't drop the sarcasm I'm going to—"

"How does one collect rainbow dust?" I interrupted the brewing fight.

"In sieves, of course. We scoop them through a rainbow, and the fibers harvest the dust." Idris looked at me curiously. "Do you not have rainbow sieves on Alfheim, either?"

"You guys can touch your rainbows?" I balked. "How is that even possible?"

"We have rainbow sieves." Maja gave me her *idiot* look again. "You probably just don't know about them because you grew up off-realm. Midgardians lost access to their rainbows centuries ago."

"You used to be able to touch rainbows on Earth, too?" Was there no end to the day's surprises? "What happened?"

"That's a story for another day," Idris said. "We should get you inside onto the castle grounds before anyone sees you. Why are you this far out? Did you get lost?"

"Our coordinates should have put us closer," Viggo said. "The storm must have blown us off."

"We don't usually get thunderstorms this early in the summer." Idris glanced up. "Thor must be in a mood."

"Ooh." My ears perked up. "Does he visit often, or—"

"Down, girl." Maja cracked her first smile of the day.

"Shut up," I hissed.

Idris giggled. "You're picturing Midgardian Thor, aren't you? The one your home world made movies about?"

Obviously. "Yes."

"Sorry to disappoint you, but the real Thor looks nothing like that one. He's much older, with red hair, and a beard I fear hasn't been combed in centuries."

Idris sighed. "But he does have a lovely stepson—and Ull looks a *lot* like the guy from those movies."

"Oh, does he now?" My mind wandered to a *very* happy place. "And where is this Ull, exactly? Does *he* visi—"

"We're here to work," Viggo interrupted. "And we only have three days, so we'd better get started."

Right.

"Everybody hop on an animal—unless you'd prefer to fly?" Idris asked.

"I'll fly," Maja declared.

"Not me. I want to ride a unicorn!" I took Idris' offered hand, and pulled myself onto Sparkles' back behind her. "Oh, my gods, I'm on a real unicorn."

Idris grinned over her shoulder. "Viggo, you want to go with Hans?"

"Sure." Viggo stretched his wings and flew onto the back of Hans' mount.

"Maja, follow us," Idris instructed. She nudged Sparkles with her riding boot, and the unicorn took off across the meadow. I clung to Idris' quilted vest as the wind whipped at my cheeks. *I wish I'd worn more than a thin sweater.*

Second note to self: layer when traveling.

We reached the castle in no time, and trotted across the wide, rock bridge that crossed a massive moat. I could barely see the tips of the castle above its grey, stone wall—the structure must have been set really far back. A guard appeared, and called down to Idris.

"Crown Princess, would you like me to admit the visitors, or send down a guard?"

"They're with me," she assured. "You can let us all in."

"Even the flier?" The guard scrutinized Maja. She hovered a few feet above the ground beside us, close enough to be a part of our travel party, for sure. Her all-black ensemble and petulant glare must have flagged the guard's danger-radar.

"She's with me, too. These are our visitors from Alfheim. I'm sure your department was briefed."

"Yes, Crown Princess." The guard bowed before calling over his shoulder. "Open the gates!"

The enormous, wooden doors parted, and at Idris' instruction I reluctantly slid off Sparkles' back. She did the same, taking the unicorn's reins in one hand and marching through the entrance. I glanced at Viggo, now standing beside me, and shrugged. Without a word, we followed Idris through the wooden doors and onto the castle grounds.

When I looked up, all breath promptly vacated my chest. *Holy mother of freaking gods. This is their castle?*

Vanaheim's royal residence made ours look like a hovel. It stood easily twice as tall as my grandmother's castle, and boasted a silvery white and blue color scheme that made Constance's all-grey stone façade look positively gloomy. I hadn't been wrong about the setback—the Vanaheim castle was positioned a full mile behind each of the four guard walls, and multiple gardens were nestled at varying intervals around each of the three sides I could see. Idris walked us past a lavender maze, through which children chased each other. The sound of their laughter mingled with the sweetly scented air to create a cloud of happiness. Beyond the lavender stood two orchards, one thick with blossoming trees, the other bearing some kind of citrus fruit.

"The work buildings are around the back," Idris said over her shoulder. "The stables, barn, smiths' shops, most of the—oh, there you are."

"I hope you enjoyed your ride, Crown Princess." Three men dressed in white approached our group. Their knee-high boots and fitted vests made me think they must have been the unicorn's keepers. My theory was confirmed when Idris handed Sparkles over to the tallest of the three.

"I enjoyed it very much, thank you." Idris smiled. "Will you check Sparkles' right front hoof? Her gait was off, I think she needs a new shoe."

I glanced down, noticing for the first time that each unicorn wore a pair of shiny, golden horseshoes. The sheen just barely peeked out from beneath the animals' sparkling hooves.

"Oh, dear." The tall groom frowned. "Were you hurt?"

"I'm a strong rider, Magnus." Idris waved her hand. "I can handle a few missteps."

"Of course," Magnus said quickly. "Were there any other issues on your ride?"

Idris tilted her head. "Well, Barry spooked when we

stopped to get a drink at the lake—the fish must have been too close for his liking."

"Were you thrown?" Magnus turned to one of the twin guards.

Stoic silence was Jans' only response.

"He was fine," Idris answered. "Just give Barry a thorough look over—he may need an extra dose of rainbow dust to soothe any residual nerves."

"Right away, Crown Princess." Magnus bowed to Idris. He and the other grooms led the unicorns past a vast daffodil garden. Barry looked longingly at the blooms as he walked away.

"The family wing is this way." Idris pointed to the right side of the castle. "It's faster if we go in the side door. Come on."

We followed her around the gardens, past families playing catch on a grassy field, and two teenagers taking what looked to be an awkward, romantic walk. I laced my fingers through Viggo's and squeezed lightly, grateful we'd passed that stage in our relationship long ago. Unwanted mate marks aside, it had been a fairly easy transition from hate to like to . . . whatever we had now. I didn't need the Norns to tell me that Viggo was a great boyfriend. He challenged me in all the best ways, pushing me to be a better *Verge*, student, and leader. He was my calm when I needed it, absorbing all my stress so I could focus on what I needed to do in any given day. He'd been my rock over this past year of craziness.

Even if he had gotten jealous of Thor's stepson.

Snort.

"This is it." Idris nodded as two uniformed guards opened the castle's side door. She walked inside, then turned and gestured for us to follow. "Welcome to the royal residence."

"Holy *skit*," Maja swore. "This is your house."

"*Ja*." Idris stepped aside, affording me a view of her not-so-humble abode. A grand staircase stretched from the polished, marble floor to the second-story balcony, where life-sized statues stood at intervals across the walk. Floor-to-ceiling windows let in almost blinding-levels of light, and what appeared to be priceless works of art adorned the all-white walls. Twin chandeliers hung from the ceiling, their crystals sparkling so fiercely I wondered if they might actually be diamonds. Idris' residence was opulent, and grandiose, and somehow, at the same time, homey.

And we got to stay here for three days?

"Your rooms are on the third floor, adjacent to the family wing." Idris' footsteps echoed off the marble floor as she crossed to the staircase. "Let's get you settled, and then we can talk over brunch."

"Sounds good. I'm always hungry." As if on cue, Viggo's stomach rumbled.

"Can't take you anywhere," I teased.

"How many residents does this building have?" Maja rested her hand on the polished banister as she climbed the stairs.

"There are around a hundred full-time—my parents and I, our household staff, and our key government officials and their families." Idris hung a right at the top of the stairs, and walked down the statue-lined hallway.

"And is it only the residents who have access?" Maja continued.

"No. We also house our governmental offices here, and those staffers account for another hundred or so bodies with clearance." Idris approached two guards who framed a shiny, oak door. They opened it at her nod, allowing us to slip into a two-story sitting room. Another chandelier hung from the high ceiling, and a slightly less ostentatious staircase extended from the room's far end.

"Welcome home, Crown Princess." A middle-aged woman in a grey skirt-suit stood behind a glossy, mahogany desk. "Your parents are out for their morning ride, but they'll join you and your guests for dinner this evening."

"Thank you, Narissia." Idris nodded, and the woman sat back down. By the time we reached the staircase, she'd resumed reading whatever document sat atop her desk.

"My protocol advisor," Idris whispered as we climbed. "She oversees my day-to-day schedule, and makes sure I don't embarrass the crown any more than usual."

"Yeah, right." I followed Idris down another long hallway. "I can't picture you *ever* embarrassing yourself."

"Oh, it happens." Idris chuckled. "I lost Freya's cat, remember?"

"Freya, the Goddess of Love?" Maja's jaw unhinged. "You met her?"

"She and my mother are friends. She stays with us for a week every spring." Idris led us to a door at the end of the hall. She opened it, and motioned for us to go through. "We thought you'd be most comfortable in here. This suite has three individual rooms, each with an in suite bathroom, and a shared living area."

"This is *gorgeous*." I let out a whistle as I walked into the living room. Twin couches and arm chairs framed a low, glass table, and a six-person conference table was positioned in front of a window that took up an entire wall. A fireplace was nestled into the second wall, and the third hosted a kitchenette. The entire room was done up in creams and whites, with pale blue accent blankets and pillows positioned around the sitting area.

"Seriously." Viggo poked his head through an open door I assumed led to one of the bedrooms. "Is this one mine?"

"It is." Idris smiled.

"I love the view." Viggo stepped inside. "And the . . . jerky tray?"

"I heard you liked dried meat," Idris said.

"I do," Viggo called from inside. "But I'm not so big on dresses, so . . ."

"Oh!" Idris laughed. "I had our staff bring up a traditional outfit for each of you for tonight's dinner.

My parents are into protocol, and Aura told me you'd be traveling light."

"Your men traditionally wear . . . gowns?" Viggo emerged from his room holding a knee-length silver robe. It was a near-identical color to his wings.

"Over their slacks, yes." Idris fanned out the fabric. "The sash ties around your waist, and knots in the back. I had our seamstress cut out holes for your wings —I hope it fits."

"I'm sure it'll be *perfekt*. Thanks, Idris." I glanced at the other two doors. "Which one is mine?"

"The one in the middle. I figured you'd prefer to be flanked by your security."

"I'm not her security," Maja said drily, at the same time as I blurted, "Viggo's *not* my security."

"Aura can take care of herself," Viggo assured Idris. "We're just along for the ride."

"Very well." Idris gestured to the kitchenette. "Our staff stocked the cabinets with all of your favorite foods."

"How'd you know our favorite foods?" I asked curiously.

"Your protocol advisor sent over a *very* detailed briefing," Idris said.

Of course she did.

"Get settled while I clean up from my ride. I'll come collect you for brunch in half an hour." Idris pointed to a small button by the main door. "If you forgot anything, this activates a data pad that links to our household staff. Whatever you need, just let them know."

"Thanks, Idris." I clasped her hands in mine. "We really appreciate your hospitality."

She grinned. "Us crown princesses have to stick together."

"While you're sticking together, I'm going to comb through some of your security footage." Maja sat down and activated her wrist com. "Oh, good. Someone's already authorized my sequence to access the files."

"My advisor is nearly as efficient as Aura's." Idris' eyes twinkled.

"Lucky you," Viggo said drily. "See you, Idris."

"Enjoy." Idris squeezed my hands, and slipped into the hallway.

I closed the door behind her. "This is nice."

"I'll say." Viggo walked over to the window. "You can't beat the view."

I crossed the room to stand beside him. We were just high enough to see not only the topiary garden below us, but also the field of wildflowers that stretched beyond the castle wall. Feathery treetops dotted the horizon, where green met with grey. Thick clouds still hovered overhead. I had no doubt we'd have an epic view of the approaching storm, if we didn't have business to attend to.

"We should take more diplomatic trips," I declared. "It's important to build relationships with our allies. Plus, this is a *really cool suite.*"

"Huh." Maja spoke up from behind me. I turned to

find her sitting on the couch. A hologram of a document projected from her com.

"What?" I asked.

"There was another unauthorized entry early this morning—just before we got here." Maja swiped the hologram to the right. The document shifted into what appeared to be surveillance footage.

"Is that the specter?" I hurriedly moved to sit beside her.

"It could be." Maja tapped the hologram, and the footage began to play. A shadowy figure hovered in front of a row of topiaries.

"Was it down there?" Viggo pointed out of the window.

"Can't tell." Maja frowned. "But wherever it was, it managed to corner her."

She tapped the hologram again. It froze on the image of a woman with long, white-blond hair. She wore a full-skirted dress, and carried a basket laden with wildflowers.

"Zoom in on her face," I instructed.

Maja placed her fingertips to the hologram and slowly drew them apart. The woman's arched brows, parted lips, and flushed cheeks suggested she'd been caught off guard.

"She's conscious," Maja deduced. "She sees the specter, and she doesn't know what to make of it. It hasn't altered her memory yet."

"Scan that image and send it to Idris," Viggo said. "We need that girl brought in for questioning."

"If her memory's been wiped, she won't be able to tell us anything," I said.

"She will if I can override whatever blocker that shadow put in her head." Maja tapped on her communicator. "Idris should have the image in a minute. I took this footage from the castle's internal feed, so hopefully we're not the only ones who picked up on it."

"I'll follow up." I typed a message on my own com, asking Idris to have her guards locate the girl from the hologram, and bring her to us at their earliest convenience. "This is good—if the specter was here this morning, he has to be close."

"And if he's close, we may have a shot at capturing him." Viggo leaned over the back of the couch. "Zoom in on him, Maja."

Maja extracted the shadow from the hologram. She swiped her hand, and the specter expanded so his image filled the space above the coffee table.

"It's scrambled," she said in frustration. "It's reading almost like soundwaves."

"What if it is?" I asked. "What if he's not actually here—he's only projecting a resonance?"

"A resonance capable of wiping memories?" Viggo rubbed his jaw. "Is that possible?"

"I have no idea." I shook my head. "But we're about to find out."

"WELCOME, VANESSA. PLEASE TAKE a seat." Idris gestured to an empty chair. She, Viggo, Maja and I were lined up on one side of the table in the first-floor conference room. The royal guards had located the girl from the hologram, and she stood in the doorway, wringing her hands together. At Idris' instruction, she shuffled across the floor. Her eyes looked anywhere but at us.

"Do you know why you're here?" Idris asked when Vanessa took her seat.

"No, Your Majesty." The girl ducked behind a wall of white-blond hair.

"Are you sure about that?" Maja pressed.

Vanessa's eyes widened. "I would never lie to the Crown Princess."

"We'll see," Maja muttered.

Vanessa shifted uncomfortably in her seat.

"Vanessa," Idris said calmly. "What is your position in the royal household?"

"I work in the kitchens. I'm a baker."

"And can you please tell me what your daily duties entail?" Idris asked.

"I awake before dawn and bake the breads, scones, and rolls served at breakfast. The first run is usually complete around sunrise, at which time I visit the gardens to pull flowers for the trays being delivered to various rooms." Vanessa's eyes darted to me. "Some of our residents eat in the main hall while others prefer to dine alone."

"I see." I made a note on the pad in front of me. "And is that where you were this morning at approximately six thirty? Picking flowers?"

"Yes, miss." Vanessa's gaze shifted from me to Viggo to Maja. "Apologies, Crown Princess. I'm not familiar with these members of the household."

"They're friends of mine, here to help us," Idris said. "You may speak candidly with them."

"Very well." Vanessa shifted in her chair. "After I selected the flowers for the trays, I returned to the castle. On my way, an old man approached me. He said he had a message from my boyfriend."

"Your boyfriend?" Maja said sharply.

"Yes, miss." Vanessa's cheeks pinked. "He's a member of the royal guard. We've only just started seeing each other, and since he's away training with his regiment, I wasn't expecting to hear from him."

"Mm-hmm. And what was his message?" Maja asked.

"I . . ." Vanessa's eyes clouded over. "I don't know."

"What do you mean you don't know?" Viggo pressed.

"I don't remember what Bjorn's message was . . . or if I even heard it. The next thing I remember is prepping the trays for room delivery." Vanessa bit down on her bottom lip. "Why? Is Bjorn in some kind of trouble?"

I studied Vanessa carefully as she wrung her fingertips together and raked her lip between her teeth. If she was acting, she was awfully good at it. "You really don't remember anything about the message? What did the old man do after he delivered it to you?"

"I . . . I don't know." Vanessa frowned. "Now that I think on it, I don't even remember what he looked like. Only that he was old."

Maja leaned back in her chair. "So, you want us to believe that you met a man whose features you can't remember, and received a message, the details of which you can't recall?"

"I know it sounds crazy," Vanessa apologized. "But it's the truth. Is Bjorn all right? If he was hurt, you'd tell me, wouldn't you?"

"We don't know anything about Bjorn," I answered. "Though it wouldn't be a bad idea to question him, too."

"On it." Viggo typed on his com.

"Are you *sure* you can't remember anything about

the old man?" Maja pressed. "Think hard."

Vanessa's features scrunched up. She was quiet for a half minute before she finally shook her head. "I'm sorry. I can't."

Maja placed her palms flat on the table. She tilted her head, appraising Vanessa with her silent stare.

"I promise I'm not lying," Vanessa whispered.

"I know you're not. Quiet." Maja continued her stare down.

I'd been on the receiving end of Maja's scrutiny, and I knew how uncomfortable it could be. But this was next-level intense.

To her credit, Vanessa remained still until Maja finally released her from her eye-lock.

"He's old, but he has his faculties about him," Maja announced. "He moves swiftly for his age, and speaks with authority. He's likely someone in a position of great power, wherever he's from. But he's desperate. His energy reads as dark, which means he's likely from Muspelheim, Jotunheim or Svartalfheim."

"Or Helheim," Viggo added.

"Helheim's curse precludes off-world travel." Maja waved her hand. "Only Hel herself can authorize release, and that's practically unheard of."

I stared at Maja. "Did you get all that just by scanning her?"

"That," Maja confirmed, "and more. Vanessa, you value your position in this household. You take pride in your work, and you would never knowingly betray the crown."

"Never," Vanessa said vehemently.

"You are dismissed." Maja turned to me. "Unless you have further questions?"

"Uh . . ." I caught Viggo's eye. He shook his head, and I turned to Vanessa. "Thank you for your time, Vanessa."

The girl looked up at Idris. "Am I in trouble?"

"No," Idris said kindly. "I appreciate you being honest with us. And I appreciate your service to this household. My parents and I *adore* your scones."

Vanessa's eyes lit up. "Thank you, Crown Princess."

Idris raised her hand, and one of the guards stepped forward to escort Vanessa from the room. The girl bowed at the door before darting outside with a heavy exhale.

"Well, that was interesting." Idris turned to Maja. "You're a reader?"

"I can read energies, if that's what you mean." Maja shrugged. "There never was a message from the boyfriend. The old man just wanted to hold her attention long enough to entrance her. Once she was under, he intended to run a retinal scan so he could replicate her key to the castle."

"So he *did* want to make a copy of her eyeball?" My stomach churned. "Ew."

"You're telling me." Idris shuddered.

"No, it's good information." Viggo leaned forward on his elbows. "The fact that he didn't get the access he wanted means he must need a fair amount of time to run that retinal scan—time he didn't get, since he was interrupted. And since an eye scan was his goal, it also means he doesn't know about the secondary scan—the crystal-lock thing Finna and Jande worked out. Have you implemented that policy yet?"

"We only just got the briefing." Idris drummed her pink fingernails atop the table. "We've barely had time to match crystals to our senior officials—those with the highest security clearance."

"It's better than nothing, but you'll need to move faster." Viggo glanced at me. "Finna and Jande offered to come and help make the matches. In light of today's breach, I'd advise you to call in any reinforcements you have available—including our team, if you want them. We're at your disposal."

Idris nodded. "I'll reach out to our scientists, and see what kind of assistance they need. I'm sure they'd be grateful for your friends' help."

"In the meantime, we need to make a list of everyone who knows Vanessa's morning routine. And of everyone who knows about her relationship with that guy. The specter hasn't been able to breach the castle yet, but he did know what to say to Vanessa to get her to talk to him. Which means he's either a mind reader—and those are rare in the dark realms—or he has someone on the inside giving him information on personnel. Things like schedules, relationships—you get the idea."

"If he has someone on the inside, why don't they just let him in the castle?" I asked. "Why would he have bothered using Vanessa?"

"Maybe they don't have the level of clearance he needs." Viggo stroked his jaw. "The bakers have access to the private residences, don't they? So they can make deliveries?"

"They do," Idris confirmed. "My gods, do you think this specter was trying to get to one of the residents?"

"I have no idea," Viggo said grimly. "Can you think of anyone who has a bone to pick with your family? Or with anyone else living in the castle?"

Idris' eyes widened. "Are you thinking someone betrayed us?"

"I'm saying that somebody's passing intel to this specter. The briefing said your last breach targeted a young staff member too—another girl with access to the residences, if I'm correct."

"Yes," Idris whispered.

"He's trying to get to someone who lives in the castle," Viggo concluded. "The question is, who?"

"And why?" I fingered the end of my braid. "What's his end game?"

"We won't know without more interviews." Maja turned to Idris. "Draw up a list of everyone you've fired, transferred, or passed up for a promotion in the past year and a half. I'll scan each of them remotely, and we can bring in anyone who reads as suspicious. We've only got three days, so we'd better get moving."

Idris pressed her fingertips to her data pad. It glowed to life, and she began typing. "I'm looping Narissia in," she explained. "She's more familiar with the dynamics of the staff than I am."

"Are you sure you can trust her?" Maja asked.

"With my life," Idris said confidently. "She's been with our family since before I was born. She'd never betray us."

"Someone's working against you." Maja stared at the ceiling. "And until we figure out who, it's best to keep things close to the vest."

"Meaning?" Idris asked.

My eyes met Viggo's, concern coursing between us.

"Meaning you are to trust no one," Maja said firmly. "And keep your guards around you at all times. Somebody wants inside this castle. And until we figure out why, we're all at risk."

We spent the rest of the day finalizing our list of potential traitors. We broke for dinner with Idris' parents, donning our traditional costumes for the white-gloved table service that apparently was the norm for the royal family's end-of-week meal. Back on Midgard, Friday night had been pizza and movie night for Elin, Larkin, Signy and I. I guessed every family had their own traditions.

After dinner, we'd issued summons to our shortlist of interrogees. They were to appear in the conference room at twenty-minute intervals starting at nine o'clock on Saturday morning. Hopefully, we'd get a few leads out of all of this . . . or better yet, an answer. Who was helping the specter?

My feet felt like lead as we trudged back to our suite. Idris left us at our door, yawning as she walked to her own suite at the end of the hallway. I followed Maja inside, struggling to keep my eyelids open with each sluggish step. Despite my physical exhaustion, my mind buzzed with energy . . . and questions. *So many questions.* By the time Viggo closed the door behind us, Maja was already in her room.

"You want a hot chocolate?" I called after her.

"I want to sleep," she called back. "Good night."

"Night!" I moved into the little kitchen, and turned to Viggo. "Cocoa?"

"Why not?" He sat at one of the stools that lined the granite countertop. "Man, what a day, huh?"

"Tell me about it." I rummaged around until I'd found a pan, milk, and cocoa powder. I flicked the lighter on the stove, measured out two servings of milk, and poured them in the pan to simmer. As it heated, I pulled mugs from the cupboards, and set them on the counter. "Tomorrow we get to interrogate unsuspecting staff."

"Yeah, but that's tomorrow's problem. Tonight, we appreciate being in a brand-new place . . . and we take in that amazing view." He pointed toward the window. The moon was so full, it easily took up a quarter of the frame. And the stars were so abundant, the sky was equal parts black and blinding white. I stared at the scene, mesmerized, until the bubbling milk rumbled.

"Oops." I pulled the pan from the burner, and stirred in a generous amount of cocoa powder. Then I filled two mugs, handed one to Viggo, and walked into the sitting area. "Couches?"

"Sure."

Viggo dropped onto the one facing the window, and patted the cushion next to him. "Come here, *Glitre*."

Careful not to spill my drink, I nestled in beside my boyfriend. I tucked my feet underneath me, and leaned into his side. "Have you ever seen that many stars?"

"Definitely not." Viggo draped his arm around my shoulders. "I thought we had it good on Alfheim, but this is next level."

"Seriously." I sipped my cocoa, letting the river of chocolate slide down my throat. *So good.*

"How are you doing with everything?" Viggo asked.

"I'm not loving that there was a break-in right before we got here," I admitted. "If the specter had breached the castle, and gotten to this wing . . . and if he'd planted a bomb, or a bug, or . . ."

"We're safe." Viggo ran his thumb along the back of my neck. "But the sooner we get to the bottom of this, the better."

"Agreed."

We drank in silence for the next few minutes. When we'd drained our mugs, we set them on the glass table. Viggo swung his long legs up on the couch, and motioned for me to curl up against him. I rested my cheek on his chest, and let the day's stresses melt away as he set his palm against the small of my back. *Mmm.*

"The circumstances aren't great, but I'm still glad

we're here," I admitted. "It's been so tense back home, with everyone trying to learn their new roles on the cabinet, and graduation coming, and finals, and . . ." My voice dropped to a whisper. ". . . my coronation."

"Yeah." Viggo nestled his chin on the top of my head. "You have a lot on your plate right now."

"You do too," I offered. "All of those things affect you."

"Yeah, but not in the same way. The role of ruler doesn't fall on my shoulders. I'm just here to support you."

"But it will someday," I countered. "You know, because we're . . ."

"Mated." I heard Viggo smile over the word. "Saying it out loud doesn't mean we have to do anything about it. You know that, right?"

"Maybe."

We didn't talk about our mate marks often. Viggo knew they scared me—the irrefutable permeance of the Norn's wing tattoos that decreed us a *perfekt* match. After the initial shock had worn off, he'd taken the revelation in his stride. Whereas I still hadn't gotten used to the idea of having a predestined mate . . . even one who was clearly a solid partner.

Viggo shifted, leaning his head so he could look me in the eyes. "Things *are* changing, though. We should probably start thinking about what we want our next chapter to look like."

"Can't it just stay like this?" I begged. "Simple, and direct, and uncomplicated?"

"It can be whatever we choose to make it," Viggo said easily. "It's you and me. Always. Nobody gets to make the rules but us."

Breath rushed from my lungs. "Good."

"But things outside of you and me are changing. You're going to be queen. I'm your minister of defense. We're going to be *Verge* Keys together. We'll have new residences, new jobs, new responsibilities." Viggo stroked my hair. "It's all coming at us."

"I know." I worried my bottom lip. "How do we navigate all of that without losing ourselves in the process?"

Viggo used his thumb to free my lip from my teeth. "Same way we always have, I guess. We take it one day at a time."

"And we promise to talk through whatever life throws at us," I added. "No matter how stressful it gets, we need to always have each other's backs."

"I'd expect nothing less."

I angled my chin up to brush my lips against his. Viggo deepened the kiss, quickening my pulse and leaving me lightheaded. But all too soon he pulled away, and exhaustion once again overtook me.

"You need to get to bed," Viggo said huskily.

"One more minute like this." I nestled my cheek to his chest and let my eyelids drift closed. "Just. One. Minute . . ."

CHAPTER 7

THE NEXT DAY STARTED with a literal bang. I awoke with a jolt, bolting upright and scanning the room to identify the sound's source. Our suite's living area glowed with the dim light of dawn, muted pink sunbeams filtering through the window wall. Viggo remained sprawled on the couch, one inky black wave hanging over his forehead, and his arm flung over his eyes. The rest of the room was still, which meant I'd either dreamed the noise or—

A second bang pulled my attention to the kitchenette.

I climbed over Viggo and dropped into a fighting stance. "Who's there?"

"It's me, you idiot." A disheveled head peeked over the counter.

"Maja?" I lowered my fists. "What are you doing?"

"Trying to make coffee. But this kitchen's an organizational nightmare." She stacked two frying pans—

apparently the source of the noise—onto the countertop.

I glanced at Viggo, who'd rolled onto his side. Heat flooded my neck as I realized we'd fallen asleep on the couch . . . and that Maja was there to witness my walk of shame. Well, semi-shame. Nothing had happened—our exhaustion had seen to that.

"Here. Let me help you." I padded into the kitchen, and put two small pots on the stove. I measured milk into one, and water into the other. Then I rummaged through the cabinets for ground coffee beans, and cocoa powder. "I've never made coffee like this—Signy had a coffee-maker back on Midgard. But there's probably some kind of a strainer or press in one of the cabinets—check up there and I'll get the mugs."

Maja peered into the cabinet over the sink. "Is this a strainer?"

I turned around. "Yes, but for pasta. Have you never made coffee before?"

"We do it differently in the colony." Maja pulled out a steamer. "This?"

"Nope." I set three mugs on the counter, and nudged Maja out of the way. I peered into the cabinet, and extracted what looked like a high-tech French press. "This should work."

"Oh."

"So how do you guys do it?" I asked.

"We're a colony of *älva*." Maja shrugged. "We do a lot of things by magic."

Right.

While I finished making our drinks, Maja leaned against the counter. "So. What's the deal with you two?"

"Huh?" I turned my head to find her looking at Viggo. "Oh. Uh . . ."

"You're bright red."

"Shut up!"

Something that looked suspiciously like a smile played at Maja's lips. "Fine. I won't embarrass you. Much."

"Just take your coffee." I thrust the mug at her.

"Thanks." She raised her drink to her lips. "Just so you know, he's really into you."

"I know." I hid behind my cocoa.

"He'd do anything to protect you. And he's completely devoted to you, though he knows you have to be the one to set the pace in your relationship. What exactly is it about him that scares you?"

"I never said he scares me. Hey, are you scanning me?" I narrowed my eyes.

"Maybe." Maja sipped her coffee. "You brought me here to evaluate threats. The psyche of the queen could be a big one."

"Well my psyche is threat free, thank you very much. And for your information, I'm not scared of Viggo. I'm scared of being locked into a lifetime partnership because of some wing tattoos I didn't choose to get."

"Excuse me?" Maja's brows arched.

"Viggo and I are mates—the Norns chose us for

each other before we were born, and marked us with these so we'd know once we found each other." I shifted my cocoa to one hand and reached up with the other to tweak the tip of my wing. "They weren't wrong—Viggo's an awesome teammate, and I know he's going to make a great co-*Verge* Key. But . . ."

"But?" Maja prompted.

"But normal teenagers get to date. They don't just *know* the first guy they ever looked twice at is the guy who's going to be their future husband . . . and their realm's king consort."

"You're scared because you didn't get a choice?" Maja guessed.

"No. I don't doubt for a minute that Viggo's the one for me." I stared into my cocoa. "What I'm scared of is that the pressure of what we're fated to be to each other is going to be too much for us. That it'll make us implode before we've even had a chance to start."

"You two seem pretty good together." Maja took another drink.

"We are," I agreed. "But we've been living in a bubble. Everything's laid out for us at the academy. We go to class, we hit the dining hall, we go back to our dorms and study, we do our *Verge* training . . . It's gotten a little crazier this year as we've integrated our new jobs, but nothing like it'll be after we graduate and I become a full-time co-regent, with Viggo as my minister of defense. The future of the realm will rest squarely on us, and with Narrik still out there, and this specter hitting Vanaheim, and with our moving residences and upping duties and—"

"Hey." Maja set her cup down and stared at me intently. "That boy adores you with every fiber of his being. He would do anything—*anything*—to make you happy. Including pretending you're not mates, and you're just dating so you realize you actually *do* have a choice in who you spend your life with. Which you do, by the way. And you don't have to be a mind reader to see that you choose Viggo."

I flushed.

"You two are good. Trust me. You just have to get out of your own way."

"Thanks, Maja." The heat slowly crept back down my neck. "Never thought I'd have this talk with you."

"Yeah, well." Maja shrugged. "I'm full of surprises."

A yawn from the couch pulled my attention to the living room. Viggo pushed himself up on one elbow. I turned back to Maja.

"We speak nothing of this," I hissed.

She mimed zipping her lips. "Wouldn't dream of it."

"Morning." Viggo swung his legs over the couch. "Somebody made coffee."

"She did." Maja jabbed her thumb at me. "I tried, but it didn't go so well."

"Thanks, *Glitre.*" Viggo stood and stretched his arms over his head. His tank top rose with the movement, giving me a peek at his taut stomach muscles. *Mmm . . .*

"You two lovebirds slept well." Maja's eyes twinkled.

I shot her a glare. "I thought you said you wouldn't embarrass me!"

"I said I wouldn't embarrass you *much*," Maja clarified.

"Well, shove it. And go get dressed. Interrogations start in an hour."

"Fine." Maja rinsed her cup and headed toward her room. I poured Viggo a cup of coffee, and carried it over to the couch.

"Hey," I said as I passed him the steaming mug.

"Hey, yourself." His morning voice was even deeper than usual. He sipped the drink. "I can't believe I passed out here last night. What time did you go to bed?"

"I didn't." The heat returned to my neck. "Maja woke me up when she was trying to make coffee."

"Really?" Viggo's brow quirked. "So, you and I . . ."

"You and I need to get ready for the interrogations." I turned toward my room, but Viggo's hand around my wrist stopped me.

"Hey," he said softly. "We're still taking us at our own pace. Nothing's changed just because we were both drained and passed out."

"I know." I turned back to face him. "And just so you know, I'm really glad the Norns chose you to be my mate."

Viggo tilted his head. "You never use that word."

"Yeah, well." I shrugged. "Maybe I should."

Viggo's dimple popped. "Maybe you should."

"I have to get ready." I slid my hand from Viggo's and scurried into my room. As I showered, I forced myself to focus on the task at hand. There was a traitor in Vanaheim, and we had a full day of interviews ahead of us.

I needed to get my head in the game.

The first round of interviews proved fruitless. The kitchen staff vehemently denied having spoken to the specter—and since they all passed Maja's scans, they were either really good liars, or they were telling the truth. The second and third rounds didn't go any better—the housekeepers and groundskeepers all came out clean. It wasn't until after lunch that we finally had a breakthrough. Vanessa's sister, Cara, mentioned that Vanessa's ex-boyfriend had taken their breakup hard. He'd missed a few days of work, and had been skipping out on get-togethers with his friends.

"How do you know this?" Idris asked. "Did you hear it from your sister?"

"No, from my boyfriend," Cara said. "He works in the stables with Magnus."

"Magnus . . ." Maja frowned. "How do I know that name?"

"You met him yesterday," Idris said. "He collected our unicorns when we rode in."

At the mention of the unicorns, Maja sat straight up.

"I knew it," she said suddenly. "Something was off

about his questions. They were too specific—slightly forced."

"His questions?" Viggo turned to his cousin.

"He asked Idris if she'd been hurt on her ride. The way he said it, it seemed like he expected her answer to be yes." Maja crossed her arms.

Idris shook her head slightly, then set her attention on Cara. "Thank you for entrusting us with this. It's proven most helpful to our realm."

"Of course, Crown Princess." Cara bowed before being escorted from the room.

The moment she'd gone, Maja leaned forward on her elbows. "We need him in here immediately—before he gets wind of what we're doing."

"Magnus is smart." Idris frowned. "If he *is* involved in all of this, summoning him will just tip him off. We need to go to him."

"Then what are we waiting for?" Maja pushed her chair back and jumped up. "Let's go."

Idris, Viggo and I stood.

"I'll have Hans and Jans come with us, just in case." Idris typed a message on her com, then glanced at me. "I've known Magnus for a long time. His father was my parents' chief groom, and Magnus worked hard to earn his title when he retired. I'd be extremely surprised if he was found to have betrayed the crown."

"I'm sorry we have to question him," I said quietly. "I know how it feels to be betrayed."

Viggo placed a supportive hand on the small of my back.

"It comes with the job, right?" Idris smiled sadly. "Nobody ever said being crown princess would be easy."

Preach.

A knock at the door pulled me from my thoughts.

"You may enter," Idris called.

The door opened, and Hans and Jans stepped through. Each of them had a long, metal rod tucked into their belt.

"What are those?" I whispered.

"Shocking sticks," Idris said easily. "In case Magnus is even more compromised than we fear."

Oh, gods.

Hans and Jans moved aside, their massive forms framing the doorway. With the path clear, Idris pressed her hands together and drew a breath.

"I suppose there's no point in waiting any longer," she said easily. "Let's continue our questioning in the stables."

CHAPTER 8

"CROWN PRINCESS IDRIS. WERE you scheduled for a ride?" Magnus looked up from the stool where he sat in an open area of the barn, re-shoeing one of the unicorns. "I'm sorry, I don't have Sparkles saddled for you. But if you and your friends don't mind waiting a moment, I can have the steeds mounted up in—"

"I'm not here for a ride, Magnus." Idris waved discreetly at Hans and Jans, who hovered conspicuously close to their charge. They took two steps back, keeping their hands on their shocking sticks. "I'm here to talk to you."

"Talk to me?" Magnus picked a loose piece of rubble from the unicorn's hoof. "With an entourage?"

I bit down on my bottom lip. If we weren't there for a ride, it was pretty weird for me, Viggo, Maja, Idris and her bodyguards to be clustered around Magnus' stool. Even the unicorn was whinnying softly.

85

"Maybe the three of us should go," I whispered to Viggo and Maja.

"You're from Alfheim, right?" Magnus treated Maja to a smile. "Unicorns must seem pretty magical to you. If you want, I can take you for a ride after I finish with Firefly, here."

Maja bristled, no doubt caught off guard by his overly familiar tone. "I'm good."

Magnus shrugged. "Your loss."

Rude.

My eyes narrowed as I studied the groom. Magnus held himself with the same confident air as the guys I'd learned to stay away from back at Granite High—the players to whom everything had always come easily. The ones who inevitably exhibited diva-level melt-downs the minute life didn't go their way.

Or made a deal with mysterious, crown-betraying shadows.

"Magnus." Idris folded her hands across her waist. "Look at me."

Magnus reluctantly glanced up from Firefly's hoof.

"Have you betrayed my family?" Idris asked softly.

Magnus' jaw dropped. "Why would you ever think that?"

"Have you betrayed my family?" Idris repeated.

"I would never do *anything* to hurt you, Crown Princess." His shoulders tensed. "Or to jeopardize my position in this household. You know that."

"We've known each other for a long time," Idris said. "We were in the same fencing classes all through our primary years, and you've served as our chief groom since I came of age. In all that time, I've never seen you set a foot out of line."

"Exactly." Magnus' eyes shifted between Idris and her guards. Their hands tensed around their shocking sticks.

"What I also know," Idris said easily, "is that you've experienced a loss. Do you want to tell me about your breakup with Vanessa?"

"With due respect, Crown Princess, that's personal."

"It is," Idris agreed. "But it has recently come to my attention that the end of your relationship may have impacted the security of my household."

"I—uh . . ." Magnus' skin paled. He looked from Idris to her guards to Maja, who was putting off seriously strong angry vibes. She must have read something in her scan that confirmed our suspicions. Either that, or she *really* didn't appreciate being asked out on a unicorn date.

Snort.

"Stand back." Viggo spoke softly in my ear. "He's about to run."

"I'd like to see him try." Maja's voice was no more than a whisper.

"We can do this the easy way or the hard way," Idris said calmly. "At the end of the day, we're more concerned with who you're working with, and what they want from the crown than we are with your betrayal. Though that will be dealt with, of course."

Idris nodded at Hans and Jans, and they pulled their

shocking sticks from their belts. They stepped closer to Magnus, whose forehead now bore a thin sheen of sweat. Firefly whinnied again, her silver-blue mane whipping back and forth as she swung her head. Her horn thrust dangerously close to Magnus, who sat paralyzed on his stool. If we didn't do something, somebody was going to get hurt—either the unicorn, or her groom, or one of us.

I stepped away from the group, and ran the length of the barn. A full dozen unicorns filled the stalls, but I didn't spot another groom until I reached the second-to-last row. A middle-aged man stood inside a stall, filling a trough with a sparkling mixture of green clovers and golden . . . rainbow dust, maybe?

"Hey. You." I called over the stall door. "I need you to come and take Firefly."

"Isn't Magnus reshoe-ing her?" the man asked.

"Magnus is needed elsewhere," I said. "Come with me. Please"

The groom quickly finished pouring the mixture and let himself out of the stall. The rest of the unicorns watched curiously as we ran past them, to the front of the barn.

"Magnus?" The man looked anxiously from Idris to the shocking stick-wielding guards. "What's going on?"

"Take the unicorn," I said firmly. "Before someone gets hurt."

As if on cue, Firefly swung her head around. Her horn nicked Magnus' cheek. He jumped up from his stool, Firefly's leg still in his grip. The guards' sticks sparked. Firefly's eyes shone white. She jerked her leg free, and let out a fierce snort. Viggo grabbed me by the shoulders. He pulled me into him and whirled around, shielding me from the panicked animal. Hooves thundered as Firefly charged down the corridor. When I looked up, the groom I'd brought over had taken off after her. He shouted apologies to the Crown Princess over his shoulder.

Viggo released me, and I squeezed his bicep in gratitude. My heart thundered at the sight of Hans and Jans standing directly in front of Magnus, their shocking sticks now pointed directly at his chest.

"Like I said," Idris said calmly, "we can do this the easy way or the hard way."

Magnus' shoulders drooped, and he lowered his chin to his chest. "I'm sorry, Crown Princess."

"For what?" Idris asked.

Magnus looked up sadly. "For everything."

We spoke to Magnus for more than two hours. He didn't hold back—he told us everything about his interaction with the specter, how he'd gotten the old man past the wall guards, and why he'd compromised the safety of the family he'd sworn to protect. As it so often did, his betrayal came down to a broken heart. He and Vanessa had been going out for two years, and he'd been ready to propose when she left him for Bjorn. The next day he'd been out on a ride when an old man had approached him. The man, who'd identified himself only as 'a friend,' had told Magnus that he was a powerful magic wielder. And that, if Magnus so desired, he could help him win his love back. All Magnus had to do was get him access to the royal family. Magnus had been suspicious, of course, and made the man swear that no harm would come to the King, Queen or Crown Princess. Only then would Magnus agree to get him past the wall guards. A few days later, Magnus brought a herd of unicorns out for a free run, tucking an extra groom's uniform into his saddle bag. The old man met him in the meadow, changed into the all-white stable attire, and returned with Magnus and the herd. To the guards, he appeared to be just another groom wrangling a group of spirited unicorns. Magnus let him sleep in the stable overnight, and told him where to find Vanessa in the morning. He knew his ex-girlfriend's security clearance could get the old man the access he needed. And since the man promised he could talk Vanessa into helping him *without* harming her in any way, Magnus didn't think he needed to worry. He returned to his chores, genuinely believing the stranger would have worked his magic—and won him back Vanessa's heart—by the time breakfast was served.

Of course, Magnus' plan hadn't gone at all the way he'd hoped. When Vanessa refused to allow the old man into the castle, he'd grown angry and disappeared. Security footage showed the specter as a shadow flickering out of view, so Magnus' story aligned with the evidence we'd collected. Though it didn't help us track down the shadowy figure who'd somehow portal-ed into the realm without anyone noticing. Twice.

Magnus was taken into custody for further questioning—and likely, a stripping of *all* his security clearances. He felt terribly about what he'd done, but his remorse didn't change our threat level. Somebody was determined to get inside the castle. And we still didn't know who—or why—they were coming for the royal family.

"Someone should check in with Nidavellir," Viggo said as we left the stable. "I wonder if it's more than just Vanaheim's royalty being attacked."

"That's a good idea." I typed on my com, sending an update to Signy and asking her to follow up with the other light realms. "I'm assuming Alfheim's exempt, since my grandmother already did enough dark deeds to compromise our integrity."

"You never know," Idris said. "Now that your horrible Minister Narrik is gone, a light royal strike would likely include your family as well."

"Great." I groaned. "What do you think, Maja? Any idea who this mysterious old man is?"

My friend scrunched her nose up. "He appears as a shadow in my head, too. I can't get any more of a read on his facial features, only on his energy. But it's dark —*really* dark."

"So you think he's from Helheim?" My throat closed. "Oh, gods. Do you think Dragen escaped somehow?"

"Show me Dragen," Maja instructed.

"How?"

"Think about him—remember your interaction with him, and I'll see him through your thoughts."

"This friendship is so weird," I muttered.

But I did as Maja instructed, recalling my horrific encounter with my dark elf uncle. I'd just gotten to the part where he'd knocked Viggo unconscious when Maja announced loudly, "No. It's not him."

"Thank gods," I whispered. I released the memory, then reached out to clasp Viggo's hand.

"You okay?" he asked.

"Just don't like remembering the time you almost died." I shuddered.

"I did not almost die. I was just . . ." He glanced at the sky. ". . . uh, regrouping."

Sure. We'd go with that.

"But the specter's definitely on the same level as Dragen in terms of the darkness of his energy." Maja looked thoughtful. "And he can shapeshift, or project himself, which both require high levels of magic. There aren't many dark mages with that kind of power."

"Plus he can open an undetectable portal," Idris added. "Does that narrow the range of suspects down at all?"

"We can rule out Helheim," Viggo confirmed. "Nobody but Hel is going in or out, and if it was her she'd have blasted straight into the castle and killed whoever she was after."

"Fair." I nodded. "And we can rule out Jotunheim,

too. I just did a paper on them, and it turns out frost giants can't portal into light realms without a decompression period—something about their bodies not being able to immediately acclimate to our air pressure. Like when human scuba divers have to swim up slowly, you know?"

"I don't know," Idris said, "but I take your word for it. So that's two dark realms down. That leaves us with Svartalfheim and Muspelheim."

I shuddered. "Gods, I hope it's not Svartalfheim."

"Why? We're more familiar with them, and I'd rather the helbeast we know than the helbeast we don't."

"I guess. I just . . ." A burst of recognition shot across my brain. "Maja. You said the specter's energy was like Dragen's, right?"

"The level of darkness was a match, yes. Why?"

"What if it's someone he knows?" I whispered. "Or someone he's worked with? The Huldra, maybe, or—"

"We sent the Huldra to Helheim too," Viggo reminded me. He quickly brought Idris up to speed on everything we'd gone through almost two years ago.

"It's not the Huldra, but I see what you're driving at, Aura." We strolled into the lavender garden. Maja paused in the middle of it, and placed her hand on her hips. "Someone whose ultimate goals aligned with Dragen's would have a similar energetic resonance. You say he wanted you dead, right?"

"Yup." I carefully stepped over a patch of blooms.

"Well, who else in Svartalfheim wanted you dead?"

Maja followed me through the garden. "Any other uncles or cousins who wanted your senate seat?"

"Nope. My cousin Ondyr lives with us on Alfheim now—he just wanted out. And Dragen was the only one who wanted me dead. The rest of the family wanted me to relocate to Svartalfheim and go into the family business." I shuddered.

"Hmm." Maja stared at the sky as she walked. "Well. It'll come when I least expect it. It always does."

"So, what do we do now?" I asked.

"I don't know that there's much that we can do." Idris sighed. "Your friends are coming tomorrow to help us with the crystal matching—hopefully that'll keep the specter from coercing anyone else to do his bidding. Or at least, it'll keep him from being admitted to the castle against our wills."

"True," I said. "And you might want to get ahead of this. Issue a statement disclosing the recent security breach—without disclosing *who* compromised the crown, of course. And let everyone know you're doing everything in your power to keep them safe from *all* threats. If they know you're watching, hopefully they'll close ranks if the specter approaches any of them."

"Good idea." Idris nodded. "I'll draft that immediately, and send it out tonight. Are the three of you still planning to leave tomorrow?"

"Yeah. Unless you need us to stick around, we have to get back to school." I stuck out my tongue, and Idris laughed.

"I don't miss that schedule," she said. "Though

things were a lot easier when my only responsibilities were studying for tests and writing the occasional paper."

"Clearly, you never endured Professor Bergen's *Verge* workouts." Viggo groaned.

"No. But I did get to take a few fencing classes. I went undefeated, since nobody wanted to get in trouble for hurting the princess." Idris' easy grin was contagious.

As we made our way back to the castle, and changed into our formal dinner attire, I couldn't help but wonder what would happen after we left Vanaheim. With Finna and Jande on their way, and a new security system about to be in place, we'd taken steps to ensure Vanaheim's royal residence was at least a little safer. But the specter was still out there somewhere. And while we still didn't know who—or what—he was, something told me we were going to find out.

CHAPTER 9

WE CAUGHT THE BIFROST back to Alfheim on Sunday afternoon. We stuck around long enough to get Jande and Finna settled into our former suite. The staff had changed it over while we'd been at lunch, turning Maja's room into a science lab complete with a vast crystal display—on loan from the royal collection, apparently—and making Viggo's and my rooms over for Jande and Finna. Jande looked like a kid in a candy shop when he caught sight of the window wall and massive sleigh bed where he'd be crashing. Meanwhile, Finna ignored her room completely—she went straight into the makeshift lab, and didn't come out until I poked my head in to tell her we were leaving.

"Be safe," she said as she enveloped me in a hug. "There was an issue at the capital on Friday—someone defaced one of the statues near the main building, and a fight broke out near the senators' residences."

"Were the two incidents related?" Viggo asked.

"I'm not sure." Finna rubbed her pink crystal necklace. "But it's been a while since we've had any problems like that, so just be on the lookout, okay?"

"Will do." Viggo raised a hand at Jande, who was now gawking at the living area. "You going to let Finna do all the work here?"

"Obviously I'm going to help." Jande strolled into the kitchen. "Right after I make us some—ooh, is this *unicorn tea*? I've never seen it! It's tea, mixed with real unicorn dust—the powder their manes emit when they're transitioning from foals to adolescents."

"Like dandruff?" Maja wrinkled her nose. "I'll pass."

"It has magical properties." Jande crossed his arms. "You're telling me you don't want to imbibe the rarest of all mystical elements in pursuit of inner peace, higher learning, and awareness of one's true calling?"

Maja shrugged. "I don't need a tea for that."

"Well aren't you special." Jande arched his brow.

"She is, isn't she?" I threw my arms around Jande. "Don't get into too much trouble while you're here."

"I'll try," he promised.

"I'll keep him in line," Finna vowed.

Viggo snorted. "Good luck with that."

"Idris is right down the hall if you need anything." I released Jande, and crossed to the door. "You're sure you're okay to miss school?"

"We only had two performance exams scheduled, and both of those professors said this more than qualified for independent study. We're clear." Jande poured water into a pot, and pulled two mugs from the cabinet.

"One look at those crystals, and I can see why." Finna glanced over her shoulder, clearly eager to get back into her lab. "They have elements on Vanaheim we've never even heard of! The properties they must be able to channel here are unfathomable."

"I'm sure," I said. "Just make sure you get everyone set up with their resonance codes before you start researching the effects of unicorn horns, or troll diamonds, or whatever other crystals they've got in that collection."

Jande banged a cabinet door closed. "They have troll diamonds here? Good gods, we'll be able to *time travel.*"

"Nobody is time traveling," Finna said sternly. "You know that's beyond our security clearance."

My brows shot to my forehead. "There's such a thing as time travel?"

"Yes," Jande nodded seriously. "But the mechanism has proven elusive on Alfheim, on account of the lack of proper tools. But if they have troll diamonds . . ."

"Uh . . ." I toed the ground. "I didn't know those were real things. I just made them up."

Jande's shoulders sagged. "Why would you do that to me?"

"To be fair, it seemed like a pretty absurd combination of words."

Finna's lips quirked up. "Well, they're real. And it turns out they have *two* pairs in the royal collection."

"So, we *do* have troll diamonds?" Jande bounced on his toes.

"No time travel," Finna said sternly.

Jande transferred the now-steaming water to two mugs. He added tea balls to each, and passed a mug to Finna with a sigh. "You have to go to sleep eventually."

"That's our cue." I opened the door, and tugged Viggo after me. "Do good, both of you. But especially you, Jande."

"I am always good. Tell Ondyr I miss him already," Jande called.

"Will do."

Maja, Viggo and I left them, Bifrosting back to Alfheim in a considerably calmer transport than the one we'd taken in. After debriefing with Signy, and drafting a summary of what we knew about the specter, we ate a quick dinner and headed off to bed. Since Maja was staying in the empty room three down from mine, I walked her to her door and checked to make sure she didn't need anything.

"The telepaths can send up any items you forgot, so be sure to ask—there's a com near the door. Just push this button"—I pointed—"and whatever you ask for will appear."

"Sounds good." Maja yawned. "See you in the morning."

"See you," I said. Then, because I couldn't help myself, I turned and threw my arms around the faerie.

"Ouch. You're squishing my wings."

"Sorry." I pulled back so I could hug her more gently.

"Why are we touching?" Maja shifted uncomfortably.

"Because you're my friend," I said. "And you helped me this weekend. Thank you."

"You can thank me by *not hugging me.*"

I released her with a sigh. "One of these days, you're going to admit that you like me."

"I like you fine," Maja said. "Just never hug me again."

I turned on one heel and headed back to my dorm. "I can't promise that," I called over my shoulder.

"Try!" Maja called back.

I closed my door with a chuckle. We might never be best friends, but we made a decent team. And somehow, I knew we'd end up needing each other.

More than I could possibly imagine.

Finna hadn't been wrong about the unrest in Alfheim. As the week went on, it only continued to grow. Another defacing occurred at the capital—this time a piece of art commissioned to mark last year's return of the *Opprør* senators. And a nearby community garden burned down in the night, whether by accident or arson, we couldn't determine. The air surrounding the capital was thick with both smoke and unease. Something was brewing, and though our security teams couldn't pinpoint any outside interference, I couldn't shake the feeling that Narrik had something to do with it. He'd been quiet for too long. These seeds of discord during a period of peace couldn't have been mere coincidence.

But I couldn't think too much about the issues in the capital. I kept my nose to the books all week, spending every available moment preparing for my last *ever* set of exams. After Friday's grueling *Verge* final, I treated myself to a twenty-minute nap before I dragged my exhausted carcass out of bed and headed to the royal residence for my weekly educational meeting with Constance. As was our custom, I dressed for tea and met her in the palace garden. A table for two was set amidst the roses, its white linen cloth topped with china cups, saucers, and plates. My grandmother stood in front of the three-story fountain, tossing crumbs to the large, golden fish who lived in its bottom pool.

"Rule the realm, feed the fish," I teased as I made my way across the grass. "A regent's duties never end."

"Something you'd be wise to remember," Constance said. She turned with a small smile, and held her hand out to the table. "Join me?"

"I always do." I took my seat across from my grandmother, laying my napkin across my lap and folding my hands together the way Eunice had taught me. "So, what's today's royal lesson? The greeting protocol for foreign dignitaries? How to *not* tick off a fire giant?"

"None of those." Constance fell silent while a white-gloved waiter poured tea into each of our cups. He set the rose-patterned teapot onto a trivet, then used silver tongs to retrieve finger sandwiches from the tiered platter at the edge of the table.

Once he'd left, I raised my teacup to my lips. "Best housewarming gift for a castle dedication?"

"No, Aura." Constance met my gaze with a sad smile. "Today I want to tell you how I'd live my life if I had to do it over again."

Oh, gods.

I set my teacup down. "You're not sick, are you?"

"I've just had my physical, and now that the dust has finally left my system, I'm healthier than I've been in years." Constance raised her chin. "Thank you for asking."

"Then why such a wonk-wonk lesson?"

"Excuse me?" My grandmother frowned.

"Why are you being sentimental?" I narrowed my eyes. "It's not like you."

"No. It's not," she agreed. "But seeing as you're about to begin your reign, I'd like to encourage you to make *different* mistakes from mine."

Fair enough.

"When I was your age, I had none of the responsibilities I do now. My parents let me be young—go to school, travel the realm, find my sense of purpose in my own way. Security was always an issue, and I had to take care not to put myself or Alfheim at risk. But I had freedoms you never will, for far longer than I had any right to. My parents ruled our realm until I was much older than you are now, and when they passed away, I was well prepared to step into their shoes. Or, so I thought."

Constance sipped her tea, and I took the opportunity to sample one of the finger sandwiches on my plate. My nose wrinkled as the distinctive taste of dill weed hit my tongue. *Blech.* I discreetly slipped the bite into my napkin, and shook it out beneath the table. One of the chipmunks would eat it later. *I hope.*

"So, what happened?" I asked.

"I lacked your confidence." Constance shook her head. "I'd been well trained by my parents, and I knew exactly what I needed to do to uphold the values they'd brought to their reign. But I was insecure—I'd never been comfortable with the idea of becoming queen, and I doubted my own ability to make the kinds of decisions that would affect an entire realm."

Same, Constance.

"What did you do?" I picked up a lingonberry finger sandwich.

"I outsourced too many of my duties," Constance said. "I brought in an expert on diplomacy to oversee relations between different regions on-realm. I appointed a cultural minister to uphold the traditions my predecessors had taken care to nurture. And to manage matters of day-to-day oversight, I created a position titled Minister of State. My initial selection for the role handled it admirably—I selected a member of my parents' cabinet, one I'd known my entire life, and who'd spent decades proving he had the best interest of Alfheim at heart. But . . ."

Constance's eyes dropped down to her teacup.

"But?" I prompted.

"But then he died," she said uneasily. "Very abruptly, without having ever been ill. His death was not only unexpected, but it left me scrambling to fill his position. I should have taken it over myself—I had the skills, and as the realm was at peace, the actual duties were more than manageable. But I continued to doubt myself. And when a promising young politician stepped forward to ask for the job . . . I gave it to him."

My breath hitched. "Narrik."

Constance nodded. "Fyrs presented himself admirably. At least, he did for the short time I observed him before your mother passed, and I spent those two years in solitude. You'd never have known back then that Fyrs was capable of becoming, well, what he is now. But I should have seen it. Or I should have had him thoroughly vetted by my *Empatis* before handing over that level of control. That's been my biggest mistake, Aura— and one I urge you not to repeat. I didn't trust myself to do the job. I didn't trust my own instincts. I should have been more involved—taken the reigns of my own life; my own rule; my own realm. I should have done the necessary research and made the hard calls *that were in my power to make.* I believe in destiny, and I do believe I was gifted this role for a reason. But I squandered whatever faith the Norns placed in me the moment I ceased to be an active participant in my own life."

My heart tugged. "Constance . . ."

"My other mistake was failing to rely on the *healthy* support system my parents had put in place for me. You have to be able to trust those you surround yourself with. You're going to need them, in dark times *and* in good. And make no mistake, you will face dark times. Nothing so extreme as what I put our realm through, gods willing. But there will always be an ebb and flow—some eras favor the light, and sometimes we scramble to maintain our foothold. No matter which phase we're in, my hope for you is that you've surrounded yourself with an honorable team on whom you can rely no matter what."

My grandmother spoke so earnestly, I couldn't help but feel sorry for her.

"You never had that team." I leaned forward. "Not that I saw, at any rate."

"I did in the beginning of my reign," she admitted. "My parents left me a cabinet filled with individuals who loved them, loved their legacy, and wanted to see it continue through me. They gave me all the tools I needed to thrive, but I lacked the confidence I needed to do the job. That's my own fault, and the realm paid heavily for it. Trust yourself, Aura. And trust the friends you've brought onto our cabinet. They're strong-minded, honorable souls. It doesn't take an *Empati* to see that."

"They're pretty rad." I grinned at the queen. "And I definitely trust them, a hundred percent. But I don't know that I can say the same for myself. This job's a lot. I get why you second-guessed your ability to handle it."

"I lacked your strength." Constance shook her head. "Everything was handled for me my entire life, so despite my family's best intentions, I never properly learned to stand on my own. Whereas you knew adversity from practically the moment you were born. You were raised off-realm, without the parents you deserved . . ."

I reached across the table to touch Constance's hand. "I wish I'd known my parents. There's no getting around that. But I didn't lack for love in my upbringing. Signy and Larkin and Elin . . . they're my family every bit as much as the one I was born into. They've stood by me through everything, and given me more support and chances than I had any right to expect. It may not have been a conventional royal upbringing, but it made me who I am. And I wouldn't trade them for anything."

Tears filled my grandmother's eyes. "I am sorry, Aura. I've caused you so much pain."

"You have," I said honestly. "But family's more than what you're born to. It's what you build along your journey. And even without my parents, I am beyond rich in family. I've got some of the greatest friends in all the realms. For that, I'm truly grateful."

"You should be." Constance turned her palm up so she could squeeze my hand. "I don't know that I've had a true friend since becoming queen."

"You have Eunice," I said, referencing our protocol advisor. "She seems pretty keen on you."

"She's paid to be kind." Constance shook her head. "Regardless, I want you to nurture your friendships. Trust your friends' judgment. And trust your own. You'll make a great ruler, Aura. Alfheim is lucky to have you."

I ducked my head at Constance's rare compliment. It wasn't like her to be so sentimental.

"Is everything okay with you?" I asked. "I'm not used to this kind of . . ."

Constance tilted her head in confusion.

"Usually we cover more boring things in these chats," I amended. "Which topics to avoid at a formal dinner, how to not offend the Archduke of Nidavellir by serving the right kind of goat meat, that type of stuff."

Constance smiled sadly. "I just look at you, poised on the precipice of your reign, and I want you to have every possible advantage. You stand to offer Alfheim so much more than I ever could have. I want you to make different mistakes—don't repeat anything close to mine."

"On that we can definitely agree." I squeezed my grandmother's hand again. "But don't be so hard on yourself. You've changed since I met you—we're on a good path now. And so is our realm."

"I hope so," she whispered. "And I hope you'll forge *your* own path. I know I'm vocal in my support of our traditions. And I do believe it's important to honor the past."

"If you're talking about the fancy titles at cabinet meetings, I don't think my friends and I can get on board with that."

"I understand." Constance's eyes softened. "And though I will publicly continue to assert my views—which have merit, you should know—privately, I respect that you have such a close relationship with those you've chosen to trust. And maybe this monarchy needs a bit of a royal rebel to shake things up."

I slowly lowered my teacup to its saucer. "Why, Constance, are you saying you *approve* of my style?"

The queen raised her chin. "You may draw whatever conclusion you wish."

Wow.

It was the most support I'd ever gotten from my grandmother. And as we sipped our tea and nibbled on a fresh plate of cookies, she told me about the years leading up to her reign, the days before she was hardened by loss, when she enjoyed the freedoms of a princess—and didn't have to live with the rigidity of a ruler. She told me about a trip she and her best friend took to Vanaheim—how she'd marveled at the vast herds of unicorns. And how the two of them had even caught a ride with a Valkyrie, and flown a Pegasus from one end of Alfheim to the other. For the first time in a long time, my grandmother was light, and open, and happy. She was exactly what I'd always hoped she would be.

But as much as I enjoyed our conversation, I had to get back to the academy. I had two papers to write, a briefing to complete, and a meeting to prep for. When nothing remained on our plates but crumbs, I reluctantly pushed back my chair and returned to my duties until it was time to go to bed.

The attack came while I was sleeping.

CHAPTER 10

"AURA, ELIN! GET UP! We have to get you out of here!" Signy's too-loud voice jarred me from my sleep.

"What's happening?" Elin mumbled from her bed.

"There's been an invasion. Fire's tearing through streets around the capital. The senators have fled their homes." Signy ripped the comforter off my bed, and pulled me to my feet. "Get dressed, and get moving. *Now.*"

"Oh, my gods." I leapt to the floor and rushed to grab a set of training clothes. My knees wobbled from the simultaneous shock of being pulled from my bed and discovering we were under attack. It had only been a week since I'd returned from Vanaheim, and while the unrest had continued to grow, we'd grossly underestimated the scale of the threat.

"Finna is still on Vanaheim with Jande, correct?" Signy barked.

"They aren't due back until Sunday," I confirmed. "What happened?"

"Portals opened at each corner of the governmental complex." Signy tossed a pair of boots my way, and I quickly slipped into them. "Streams of dark warriors poured through, and took over the city. We were grossly unprepared."

"*Skit,*" Elin muttered as she shoved her feet into shoes. It was a testament to Signy's focus that she didn't admonish my friend for her language.

"What are we doing to mitigate the damages?" I asked.

"I've already sent warriors to the front lines. Larkin's leading the team to collect the senators, and transport them to safety. The ground captain is commanding a unit whose sole mission is to close the open portals, and eliminate threats they find along their path." Signy retreated to the door. She peeked outside, before waving us toward her.

"And the rest of the threats?" I pushed myself to my feet.

"I have a team dealing with the dark warriors who are currently raining fire upon the capital. Move!"

"What about my grandmother?" I jogged toward the door, Elin on my heels.

"A protection unit is already at the royal residence. The queen is safe," Signy confirmed. "Another team is here at the academy, to make sure no harm comes to you or your friends. Which it won't, if you *hurry your butts up* and get down to the panic room."

"We have a panic room?" Elin whispered.

"Apparently." We ran into the hallway. "Are the rest of the students safe?"

"The residence halls are undergoing evacuations—students are being taken to the great hall. Its security is unparalleled, so I know they'll be all right there."

"But not everyone's in the residence halls." I threw my palm against the wall as I tripped over an untied lace of my combat boot. "I just saw Wynter yesterday—she and the other fourth-year *Bridgers* are doing some kind of overnight in the Cloak. What if they—"

"*Everyone* is being relocated to a secure location," Signy assured me. "Even the *Bridgers*. We have a *Protektor* with the ability to access the Cloak and retrieve them."

"Okay, but what about Bob and the rest of the animals in the *Dyr* unit? They're exposed, and—"

"We have a blanket protection already covering the academy." Signy nudged me down the stairs.

"Okay, but—"

"But nothing." Signy pulled open a door I'd never noticed in our common room. Wall sconces illuminated a downward-spiraling staircase. "Get inside. The rest of your cabinet members, minus the queen, should be here shortly."

I reached back to squeeze Signy's hand. "Be safe."

"You too." She raced from the common room, no doubt ensuring the rest of the students had cleared the dorms.

With a heavy heart, I followed Elin down the stairs.

I rounded the corner to find Viggo pacing alongside a massive conference table. His hands were balled into fists, and his shoulders were so high they practically touched his ears. When our eyes met, he exhaled heavily and raced over to scoop me into a hug.

"Thank gods." He buried his face in my hair. "Maja came down two minutes ago. Since she's on your floor, I thought . . ."

"I'm fine." I rested my palms against the taut muscles of his back. "But where's your roommate? Is Ondyr miss—"

"I'm here." Ondyr's voice echoed down the staircase. "Viggo was sent down immediately because of his job, but I stayed back to help some of the first-years get out safely. Once everyone was settled, Signy told me to come meet you guys down here."

"Thank gods you're okay." I released Viggo and flung my arms around my cousin. "What about your partner? Did you see Zara in the Great Hall?"

"She's supervising its perimeter," Ondyr confirmed. "All of the *Verge* are patrolling the area, making sure the castle's protections aren't breached."

"Good." I stepped back and wrung my hands together. "So what are we supposed to do? We're of no use to anyone down here."

"You're safe." Signy's short legs made long strides down the bottom of the staircase. She'd returned. *Thankfully.* "That's my highest priority at the moment —ensuring the safety of the rulers and the Keys."

"I'm neither," Maja interjected. "Put me to work."

"I haven't heard back from your father yet, and I gave him my word I'd keep you safe." Signy crossed her arms. "Until something changes, you're all staying here."

"Hold on." Elin raised her hand. "You said Keys. Does that mean . . ."

Oh, gods. No. Please, just no.

"Ugh. Seriously Ivy? Did you *have* to wake me up? I was having *the best dream.*" The nasally voice I'd learned to loathe on Midgard pierced the relative quiet of the panic room. Seconds later, my fear was confirmed as Britney's *Protektor* muscled her down the staircase.

"You have got to be kidding me," Elin muttered.

"Wait. There's more." I watched as the remaining Keys were paraded down the staircase. They lined the far wall of the tiny room, which now felt slightly cloying.

"Keys, I want you over there on the couches." Signy pointed to the small sitting area beneath a painting of a mountain. "Ivy, supervise them—and make sure *all* of them remain calm, and *silent.*"

"On it." Ivy arched her brow at Britney.

"What? I'm not the only one who'd rather be in her own bed. You said there's a protection around the castle, right? Why can't I just go back to—"

Britney's tirade was halted by Ivy's hand atop her mouth.

"Rude," Britney muttered.

"Cabinet members," Signy continued, "I need you to sit at the table. Now."

"What about us?" Ondyr pointed between himself and Maja. "We're not Keys or cabinet members."

"You are now." Signy grimaced. "Our minister of defense is going to need a new second. Want the job?"

"What happened to Petros?" Ondyr asked cautiously.

"We just got word he didn't survive the attack." Signy's face didn't betray so much as a hint of emotion. She'd flipped into full-on warrior mode. *Gulp.* "Which means we have an immediate opening, and a desperate need."

"I'm sorry for your loss." Ondyr bowed his head.

"As am I," Viggo said. "But Ondyr will more than rise to the occasion."

"I know he will. I trained him." Signy turned to Maja. "And I remember you said you'd rather be a consultant, but we have reason to believe these portals link throughout the realm—which means your family could be at risk, too. We could *really* use your talents on this cabinet."

Maja slid into the chair beside me. "Tell me what to do."

"I will." Signy dropped a small disc on the center of the table. She used two fingers to activate it, then extracted a holographic map from within its core. "Everyone, sit down. I need to show you what we're dealing with."

My friends did as instructed, taking seats around the oval-shaped table and staring at the pale blue image of the capital.

"The portals opened approximately ten minutes ago." Signy pointed to the swirling circles located at each corner of the governmental complex. "Assailants immediately began their attack on our realm, torching the residences before converging on the senatorial complex. The structure itself hasn't been damaged yet, but we have reason to believe it *has* been compromised. Security footage shows a shadow weaving down the hallway to the records room."

"A shadow?" My throat tightened. "Someone needs to get word to Vanaheim. Idris' family could be at risk."

"I'm on it." Viggo tapped hurriedly on his com. As he did, Signy continued with her explanation.

"Another portal opened up near the royal residence." Signy pointed to the bottom of the map. "That structure is protected with a unique blend of light magic, and so far, it hasn't been penetrated. But someone's trying to break in, and while we haven't located the perpetrator yet, it's only a matter of time before we take them into custody."

"Why?" I asked. "Why is this happening now? We've strengthened our alliance with Vanaheim, resumed sending light through the Alfheim tree, and we were well on our way to rebuilding Alfheim as a center of peace in the cosmos. What happened to make us a target again?"

"I believe you happened." Signy turned to me.

"What?"

"You're weeks away from your coronation, and

you've already shown yourself to be a leader to be reckoned with. You're nothing like your predecessor .. . which means our enemies are losing the hold they've had on our realm." Signy raised her hand to the hologram, and used two fingers to zoom in on the shadowy figure inside the capital. "Someone's been biding his time, looking for a way to reclaim his control. But you've buffered Constance with safe influences, and surrounded yourself with the best possible team. Alfheim is impenetrable. Which means he has to destroy it."

"He, who?" Maja leaned forward to study the image.

"Narrik," Viggo growled. "I'd know that monster anywhere."

"How did he get into the realm?" I demanded. "I thought we blockaded his energy signature."

"We did," Signy said. "He found a workaround. Someone's shape-shifting his form—a dark magic wielder, from the looks of it. See how the edges of his profile are slightly out of focus? That's the signature of a dark shifter."

Viggo swore loudly. "We have to kill him."

"We have to capture him," Ondyr corrected. "He's not the primary threat. Whoever shifted him is."

"And we need Narrik to identify that particular perp." I groaned. "So, let me get this straight. We capture a shadowy version of Narrik—alive, mind you. And we, what? Force him to tell us his secrets? How the hell are we supposed to do that?"

"By playing into his hand. Obviously."

I cringed at the nasally voice coming from the couch. "With all due respect, Britney, this is a cabinet matter."

"Fine." Britney shrugged. "It's your funeral."

Signy and I exchanged looks.

No, I mouthed.

She ignored me, and turned to my sworn enemy. "What are you thinking, Britney?"

"We-ell . . ." Britney drew the word over two syllables. She clearly relished the attention. "I know how Narrik thinks. I talked to those *Styra* who were working for him in the *älva* camps. And they all said his ego was his biggest weakness."

"This is not news," I muttered.

"No, but what I'm about to say will be," Britney snapped. "He has a family. One he keeps on another realm."

"What?" The entire table screeched in unison.

"Hold up." Elin raised her hand. "Are you telling me that monster found some chick to marry him? Ew."

"Marry him," Britney confirmed. "And have his kids. There are three little Narriks running around somewhere in the cosmos. Find them, hold them hostage, and I'd imagine Narrik will do whatever you want."

Horror doused my shock. "Britney, that's awful. We would never do that."

"Suit yourself." Britney shrugged. "If you don't want to win, don't play the game."

"Maybe she's on to something," Maja said quietly.

"Are you insane?" Viggo turned to his cousin. "We don't hurt kids. Period."

"Well, obviously." Maja rolled her eyes. "But think about what Britney said. Narrik's terrorized this realm, made this illogical power grab for a throne he's devalued for what reason? Because it's never been his true home."

"And that relates to his kids . . . how?" I asked.

Maja narrowed her eyes. "If we can get him deported from whatever realm his family's on—most likely the realm he's been working with—then he'll have no choice but to do what we want. He's not going to force his family to become fugitives."

"It's Narrik," I said drily. "I wouldn't put anything past him."

"Exactly," Maja said firmly. "Narrik acts in his own best interest. And if we can get him banished from *all* of the dark realms, he'll have nowhere else to go but here. None of the rest of the light realms will take him. Which means he'll have to comply with our demands if he doesn't want his family on the run forever."

Viggo and I exchanged looks. "It's logical," he said.

"True." I drummed my fingertips against the table. "But how do you get a monster banished from a dark realm? That's pretty much the purpose of dark realms —housing monsters."

"Even monsters have codes of honor." Britney spoke as if we were all slightly slow. "Fabricate proof he's broken the one of his host realm, and he's out. No questions asked."

Signy's spine straightened. "That's not a terrible idea."

"Gee, thanks," Britney snarked.

"We've determined he's working with either Muspelheim or Svartalfheim, correct?" Signy asked.

"Right." Viggo nodded. "Now that we've seen he has the same properties as the shadow that invaded Vanaheim, we know Jotunheim and Helheim are out. Any idea what the other realm's codes might entail?"

"Lucky for us, they share one cardinal rule." Signy's lips curved up. "Never betray the royal bloodlines."

"And that helps us . . . how?" Elin asked.

"The palaces of both Svartalfheim and Muspelheim are protected by a crystal." Signy leaned forward. "Their resonances project a shield that prevents anyone from entering the royal households."

"And Vanaheim's only just thinking to do this for their palace . . . why?" I asked.

"This isn't the kind of crystal a light realm would want to use." Signy shuddered. "These crystals project a dark magic that would make light creatures horribly ill. If we can replicate those crystals—in appearance only, we wouldn't want to activate them here—then we could show them to whomever Narrik's working with as proof that he'd betrayed their realm."

"It's a good plan," I admitted. "Except that our top two *Elementar* are currently in Vanaheim."

"Then we'll have to recall them," Viggo said grimly. "Professor Bergen, where could we get our hands on the kind of crystal Finna and Jande could transmute to a dark one?"

Signy glanced at the ceiling. "The only location secure enough to house that kind of element would be the royal safe. The queen's personal collection is in there—including gifts she received from dark-realm dignitaries in an effort to buy her favor."

Viggo nodded grimly. "Then that's where we'll Bifrost our ministers of science."

"I'm going too," I announced. "There's already a threat lurking around the palace—I'm not sending my friends in alone."

"You're our regent," Signy reminded me. "Protocol dictates we keep you here, *away* from the attacks."

"Oh, come on." I tilted my head. "Since when have I *ever* followed protocol?"

"I'm with Professor Bergen," Viggo said. "This kind of threat is unprecedented. Walking into it would be—"

"Look. I'm not going to ask my friends to put themselves in the line of danger while I'm kept safe in some bunker. I am *not* my grandmother. I'm not going to be the kind of ruler who sits on her butt while everyone else makes the decisions for her. I am Alfheim's *Verge Key*—well, one of them, anyway. And I am its regent—again, one of them. And I am *going* to fight alongside my friends, whether anyone in this room is comfortable with it or not." I stood and placed my palms flat on the table. "So, I suggest you all get on board, summon that Bifrost, and figure out how to get me inside the royal residence. Now."

Across the table, Elin's eyes widened in approval. Maja nodded discreetly, and Signy drew a slow breath. The room was so silent, you could have heard a pin drop.

It wasn't until Viggo pushed his chair back and stood beside me that I knew I'd made my point.

"You heard the regent," he said. "Get her into the royal residence."

The room erupted in a burst of activity. Signy set about arranging the Bifrost while Elin communicated with Finna and Jande, giving them the details of their new mission and instructing them to bring whatever materials they'd need from their Vanaheim lab to transmute a dark crystal. Ondyr, Viggo, Maja and I pulled the map to one end of the table, and began plotting out a way to get into the palace. A portal had opened nearby, and since the traveler hadn't been apprehended, its surrounding area wasn't secure. We needed to transfer directly from the academy to the palace, a process that would require Bifrost-level magic.

"But the Bifrost is impossible to miss." I shook my head. "There's no way we could get in undetected if that thing lit up the sky."

"What about *älva* dust?" Maja held up a small bag.

"Where did you get that?" I asked.

"My dad makes me swear to always carry some on me." Maja sighed. "He's so overprotective—obviously, I've never needed his help to take care of myself. You guys, however . . ."

"Can that stuff transport us?" Ondyr eyed the small, velvety satchel.

"It can," Maja confirmed. "When do you want to leave?"

I drew my shoulders back and met Viggo's steely gaze. "Now."

CHAPTER 11

THE ROYAL RESIDENCE WAS eerily silent when we dusted in. I'd brought Viggo, Signy, Ondyr and Maja with me, and once we'd assessed that the parlor outside the royal vault was secure, we moved as a team to scout the first floor. Once the Bifrost arrived, it would alert our potential intruder to our whereabouts, and our plan hinged on making sure Finna and Jande got into the vault safely.

It also hinged on our not getting ourselves killed, which was why we'd weaponed up with a generous supply from the stash in the academy bunker. Our makeshift conference room had been equipped with a weapons closet that rivaled the *Verge* facility, and each of us was draped in swords, daggers, and, in Ondyr's case, a menacing archery set. Nobody would be messing with us. We hoped.

"The east wing's secure." Ondyr's voice came from

my communicator. He and Maja had paired up to check the north and east sides of the palace.

"The west wing is too," Viggo confirmed. He and I were responsible for the south and west sides.

"Bifrost drop site is secure." Signy said through our coms. "Once you've cleared the north and south, we'll bring them in."

Viggo and I stealthily moved down the dark hallway, checking the empty offices and ballrooms. When we'd reached the meeting spot, he tapped on his com. "South wing's secure."

"And the north," Ondyr added as he approached us. "You're sure we don't need to check the other floors?"

"The ground team said the perimeter wasn't breached," Signy's voice answered. "And the queen's guards have her secured in her room. I'm calling in the Bifrost. Reconvene outside the vault."

Our coms went silent and we ran quietly toward the thick doorway at the end of the hall. We'd see Finna and Jande safely from the Bifrost to the vault, then divide up in hopes of catching whoever had opened the portal near the palace. We slipped outside, and I took my position closest to the door.

"Any minute now . . ." There was just enough moonlight to see Signy standing beside a rose bush in the castle garden.

"Incoming," Viggo said quietly.

I glanced up just in time to see a rainbow barreling into the central courtyard. It struck the ground with a thunderous boom, sending up gale-force winds that stripped the roses of petals and whipped them around the garden. Subtle, the Bifrost was not.

Finna and Jande stumbled out of the rainbow. Each clutched an overwhelming amount of what I assumed was lab equipment. Ondyr and Viggo rushed forward to help them, while Maja and I kept watch at the door. Once we were all safely inside the castle, I led my friends to the barricaded entrance to the royal vault.

"There should be a crystal inside that can pass for a dark realm protection." I spoke over my shoulder. "Find it, transmute it, and bring it to us."

"To be clear, it has to pass for both a Svartalfheim *and* a Muspelheim stone?" Jande asked.

"Correct." I nodded. "We don't know who we're dealing with, so if you can toe the line it'd help us out."

"Those realms have similar resonances," Finna spoke as she ran. "I'm sure we can make it work."

"Good. The faster the better." I positioned my eye over the scanner outside the vault. Alfheim used the same security system that Vanaheim had—a fact we intended to rectify, now that we knew specters were a thing. The scanner beeped, granting me entry, and I pulled the door open to let my friends inside. "Maja will stand guard while you work. The rest of us are going to try to track down whoever's behind this."

Finna turned around, worry lining her cherubic features. "Is it true the capital's on fire?"

"Parts of it," Signy confirmed. "But don't trouble yourselves with that—our warriors will handle the ground threat. You two just put those brilliant minds to work."

Jande placed his hand on Finna's arm. "We have to go," he said quietly.

Finna blinked back the tear that threatened to slip down her cheek. With a nod, she hurried after Jande.

"Holy mother Frigga, would you look at this place?" Jande's voice echoed from inside the vault.

"Think you can find what we need?" I called in after him.

"If I can't here, it doesn't exist!" Jande yelled back.

"Maja, secure the room," Signy instructed. "Ondyr and I will take the south perimeter, Viggo and Aura, you take the north. Let's find our perp and bring him in."

"On it." Ondyr nodded. He headed for the exit at the end of the hallway, Signy close behind him.

"It's faster for us to cut through the courtyard," I told Viggo. "Follow me."

"Deal." He jogged after me, heading outside and cutting across the sculpture garden. We were halfway through the grounds when a panicked voice rang out from behind us.

"Aura! Viggo! Wait!"

"Is that . . ." I stopped so abruptly, Viggo very nearly ran into me. I glanced over my shoulder, scanning the courtyard until I saw a woman in a white robe running awkwardly across the garden. Two massive guards trailed after her. "Is that . . ."

"Your grandmother?" Viggo's voice echoed my shock. "What is she doing here?"

"And why is she holding a sword? No," I corrected. "Two swords."

"Hold on." Viggo exhaled heavily. "Those are the Dual Swords—the magical ones crafted from the same metal as Thor's hammer, that your great-grandparents used to defend Alfheim throughout their reign. The habrók is supposed to bring them to us when we need them most, but . . . where's the bird?"

I narrowed my eyes. "And what's coming for us if we need the swords?"

"There. You. Are." Constance doubled over, gasping for breath. "I haven't. Run. In years."

Clearly.

"Why do you have those?" I pointed to the swords.

"The bird," she panted. She thrust the weapons at us, and we quickly relieved her of them. When my palm wrapped around my sword's hilt, a little *zing* shot up my arm. The blade glowed pale blue, then shot a spark at Viggo's blade in the energetic high-five I'd seen only once before.

So cool.

"What about the bird?" Viggo turned to Constance.

"He brought the swords," she answered. "I saw it outside my window. He was carrying them into the courtyard, clearly looking for you. But he was struck down by a black bolt that shot across the sky."

"Lightning?" Viggo narrowed his eyes. "There isn't a cloud out tonight."

"It wasn't the right color to be lightning." Constance shook her head. "It looked more like . . ."

A flash from my left made me crane my neck around. "Like that," I whispered.

"Yes." A low, angry voice filled the courtyard. "Put it together, *Princess.*"

"Constance, get behind me," I ordered as I dropped into a fighting stance. I shifted my weight onto my back leg, and raised my sword to eye level. Beside me, Viggo did the same. "Guards, get the queen to safety. Now."

"Oh, that won't be necessary," the voice hissed. "She's not the one I came for."

"Who are you?" I shifted slightly, scanning the courtyard for the intruder.

"The question, *Aura,* is who are you? The Princess of Alfheim, who will guide the realms to peace? Or the Daughter of Svartalfheim, who will destroy them in war?"

"No," I growled. How had my uncle escaped? "We sent you to Helheim."

"Oh, you didn't send me. *Granddaughter.*" A menacing laugh made my blood still.

"Rankin?" I whispered. *Oh, gods.*

"Correct." With that, a tall, thin man emerged from the shadows. He had the same greasy hair and narrow build as his son—the uncle who'd hired a Huldra to suck my soul. But the low ponytail at the nape of his neck had greyed with age, and his hollowed cheeks bore more wrinkles than his son's had. This was my paternal grandfather—the dark elf who'd ordered my parents' murders, and who'd vowed to fulfill the darker half of my prophesy as destroyer of realms.

This was the man who'd caused me a lifetime of pain.

This was the man I was going to rip to shreds.

"I know him." The color drained from Viggo's face. "He killed my parents."

No.

"My *Protektor*, Erik, showed me his image after my parents didn't come back from their recon mission. We were on Svartalfheim, and they'd gone to the senatorial complex to retrieve a classified document when . . ." Viggo's voice cracked. ". . . when he found them."

My heart simultaneously broke and raged. How had one monstrous creature caused so much pain?

"Listen to me, Aura." Viggo's voice was heavy with tension. "Get back in the castle. *Now.*"

"She can't hide any longer." Rankin stepped into a beam of moonlight. It reflected off his long, silver tunic and slacks, giving him the glowing appearance I'd always associated with angels. But his cruel black eyes and hate-filled stare made it clear he'd come not from light, but from pure darkness. And his set jaw and drawn shoulders made it equally clear he intended to drag me down with him. "My servant just procured her imprint."

"Imprint?" I asked.

"The tracking frequency your queen uses to keep

tabs on you." Rankin's eyes widened in feigned shock. "Oh, dear. Didn't you know?"

"I have no idea what you're talking about," I said levelly. "But I'm not hiding from you. And I'm not joining you, either. I'm going to be your end."

"Oh, *Princess.*" Rankin's smile sent chills racing down my spine. "You're going to be my crowning glory. When your father made the *unfortunate* choice to stray from his path, I thought our family was ruined. My second son didn't have the fortitude to withstand the bloodlust of politics, and my own name was so badly damaged, I may never have recovered. But then, I learned of you." Rankin crooked one finger, and something sharp hooked into my belly. I was drawn forward, a fish on a line, by a force I couldn't see.

Arugh! I winced as the invisible blade dug deep inside my gut. *How do I make it stop?*

"Aura?" Viggo kept pace at my side as I shuffled unwillingly forward. "What's happening?"

"He's a dark warrior." I gasped as the hook dug deeper in my gut. "Like Dragen."

"Well, so are you," Viggo hissed. "Fight him off."

"It's not." I grimaced as pain wracked my body. "That. Easy."

Viggo narrowed his eyes. "Then I'll kill him."

"No!" If Viggo charged, Rankin would drop him before I'd taken half a breath. "Don't give him a reason to hurt you. Stay back, and protect the queen."

"I'm not leaving you." Viggo took another step forward.

The hook dug deeper, driving a fresh wave of pain across my torso. My body lurched closer to the monster who'd killed my father.

"I'm not leaving you either," I vowed.

And with that, I dug my heels into the ground, stopping my trajectory. I closed my eyes, tightened my grip on my sword, and reached up with my other hand to clutch Maja's necklace. Then I pulled light in through my feet, and opened my aura to the darkness emanating from Rankin's black soul.

If you can't beat him, join him.

Rankin gasped as I sucked the energy from his body. The now-familiar sensation I likened to a swarm of angry bees jabbed at the space surrounding me, and I drew it in before I could change my mind. Light warred with dark inside of me, draining my strength and leaving me slightly dizzy. I carefully wove the two energies together, blending them into the double helix only dark faeries could conjure. Then I opened my eyes, released my hold on the crystal, and raised my palm.

"Go away, Rankin," I growled. "And *never* come back."

"Not without my prize," he hissed.

A grin parted my lips. "I was hoping you'd say that."

I thrust my hand forward and a beam of light burst from its surface. It struck Rankin in the chest, forcing him to the ground and releasing his hold on my gut. As the invisible hook flew from my stomach, I stumbled backward. Viggo's hand on my back kept me upright, and I drove a second beam into Dragen. And a third. But the helix was growing weaker, and as I opened my palm to deliver another blow, a black stream erupted from the ground. It flew from Rankin's hand, dark lightning carving a lethal path across the Alfheim sky. Everything shifted into slow motion as the beam shot straight up, then abruptly changed its trajectory. It spun a tight circle to travel downward, past the castle turrets and the third-floor balcony. It bore below the second-story windows, bearing a course directly for—

"Aura!" Viggo's shout jarred me from my haze. It was too late to run so I shifted into battle mode, raising my sword and preparing to deflect the black beam of death—gods willing, it could be stopped. But just before it hit my sword, something struck me from the side. I flew to the ground, my sword thumping against the dirt as I was knocked out of the way by something tall, and bony, and cloaked in the cloying scent of baby powder.

"Arugh!" My savior shrieked as the beam struck the ground. A deep boom echoed across the courtyard as the earth shook and the walls of the castle trembled. From my position on the ground I saw a stone shake loose from the balcony. It tumbled fast, splintering as it hit the wall, so its jagged edge was pointed straight down. A little nudge—that was all it would need to drive a hole straight through Rankin's twisted head. I lifted my hand, using what little energy I had left to launch the makeshift arrowhead between Rankin's eyes. But just as it was about to strike, Rankin lifted one finger and twirled it in a small circle. He disappeared in a puff of black smoke, leaving the stone to shatter into nothing.

I swore, furious that I'd been this close to destroying the monster so intent on using me to hurt our worlds. *How did he get away? And how am I ever supposed to—*

The sobbing behind me grew louder. I quickly turned around.

Oh, gods. No!

My grandmother lay crumpled on the ground. She had been the one to save me.

That act of bravery had cost her everything.

Constance convulsed as the dark beam worked its way through her body. Her legs shook beneath her long, white robe, and she crooked her fingers as if trying to stave off her pain. Her normally smooth chignon was in frizzy disarray, and her once stoic features were wracked with agony.

I crawled to her side and clasped her hands in mine. "It's okay, Constance. We'll call for a healer and—"

"No." The queen shook her head. "A dark curse isn't reversible."

"You don't know that." I rubbed my thumb along the back of her hand, trying not to stare at the dark liquid coursing through the veins. "Viggo, get on your com and get a *Kuera* here, immediately. There must be one in the palace."

"There is." A tremor overtook my grandmother's chest, and she let out a pained hiss as her veins darkened to a pure black. Whatever poison Rankin had put in her was spreading. "But she . . . cannot undo . . . this." Constance's eyes fluttered closed as she struggled to breathe.

"I'm so sorry. That blast was meant for me. You shouldn't have—"

"I have caused you . . . enough pain." Constance met my tear-filled gaze with a remorseful stare. "The least I can offer you . . . is the chance to . . . live your life."

"You saved it," I whispered.

"You saved me." The ghost of a smile glimmered on my grandmother's lips. "I didn't truly live . . . before you came along. And now . . . I want you . . . to do as I should have done. Rule with honor. With dignity. Be the royal rebel Alfheim needs."

A tear slid down my cheek. "That's what you want me to be?"

"I want you to be . . . who *you* are." Constance squeezed my hand. "Not who I, or anybody else . . . expects you to be. Live your best life, Granddaughter. *That* is my dying wish."

"Don't go." I swiped hastily at my cheek. "We're finally getting along."

Constance's raspy laugh gave way to a gurgling cough.

"What's going on?" Signy's voice burst from the southern entrance to the courtyard. "We saw the light and—oh, gods. Aura. Are you all right?"

"I'm fine," I croaked. "But Constance is . . . she's . . ."

"Who did this?" Ondyr growled.

"Rankin," Viggo said as he knelt next to me. When had he come to my side? "The bolt was meant for Aura, but the queen pushed her out of the way. She thinks what Rankin threw was a dark curse . . . and that it's irreversible."

"It is." Ondyr dropped to his knees. "I saw the black bolt—it's the deadliest affliction in my grandfather's arsenal. He used to threaten his political opponents with it. It's the reason he managed to hold onto his power in spite of everything our family went through."

"What about *älva* dust?" Hope filled my heart. "Maja's inside and I know she has some left. If we could—"

"Nothing can reverse the black bolt," Ondyr said sadly. "I'm so sorry, Aura. Your Majesty."

I looked at my grandmother—at the nose shaped just like mine, and the wings vibrating softly against the ground. At the sorrow etched in each wrinkle, and the remorse pouring from her eyes. I looked at the woman who had caused me so much hurt, who had lived through so much pain, who had just given her life to save mine. And I was overcome with heartache—for all that had happened, and for all that might yet have been.

"I'm not ready to lose you." I choked on my sob.

"I'll always be right here." Constance reached up, her trembling fingertips brushing lightly against my heart.

"Look out for me, okay?" I rested my forehead against my grandmother's. "From the other side?"

"I'll be your greatest champion," my grandmother promised. Her eyelids fluttered closed again. I held tight to her hand as her breathing grew shallow. Her chest shuddered, and another wave of coughing overtook her. Before she drew her last breath, she squeezed my hand and spoke her final words. "I am proud of you. My granddaughter. My queen."

Constance's fingers went limp. My tears streamed freely as I dropped my head to her chest and wept. I felt a hand on the small of my back, its light pressure providing what little comfort it could. A second hand touched my shoulder, and when I looked up Viggo and Signy framed me with bowed heads. Ondyr knelt nearby, his own head lowered in respect. The queen's guards wept silent tears, and even the flowers seemed to droop. The entire courtyard was somber, honoring the passing of the leader who'd driven Alfheim to its darkest days . . . but in the end, also pushed it toward a brighter future.

I would make sure her selfless act wasn't in vein.

"We got a lock on the crystal! It's right here. Now we just have to take it to . . . oh, gods." Finna's jubilant run came to a sharp halt as she looked from me to Signy to Constance. "Is she . . ."

"My grandfather killed her." Fire burned in Ondyr's eyes. "Right before he disappeared."

"I'm so sorry for your loss." Maja dipped her head.

I could only nod in response.

"Aura? Are you okay?" Jande dropped to kneel beside Ondyr.

"No. Not at all." I pulled my shoulders back. "But we're going to avenge her. And all of Alfheim. Rankin's screwed with us long enough. We need to stay off his radar long enough to find him, and ki—"

"Slight problem." Viggo's hand hadn't left my lower back. Now he rubbed small, calming circles. "Rankin said the queen had a trace on you. And it sounds like he's got that trace now, too. I don't know how, but if he has a way to track you I don't know how to keep you safe."

"I don't remember anyone asking about a trace." I shook my head.

"I do," Signy said quietly. "Regents and key personnel always have a tracking resonance coded for them. It's a security measure to deter abductions. I signed off on Aura's being done before her coronation. You were to sit for it next week."

"But I didn't," I pointed out. "So, they can't have a tracker on me."

"There are other ways to procure a code," Signy said. "Any senior level *Empati* could identify your resonance—even remotely—and code it for tracking. If someone fudged the date on my authorization, the code may already be in the private records room."

"And where exactly is that room?" Viggo asked tensely.

"The senatorial complex," Signy answered. Then she swore. "The shadow in the complex. Narrik was after Aura's code."

"And Rankin said his servant had already procured

it." Viggo picked up his sword and jumped to his feet. "We have to stop Narrik before he hands it over."

"Rankin has a head start." I folded my grandmother's hands over her chest, and picked up my own sword. "We'd better get moving."

"We'll catch him," Viggo said grimly. "I won't let you spend the rest of your life running."

"Aura's run long enough." Signy held out her hand and I took it. "Let's put an end to this once and for all."

My eyes darted to my grandmother's limp form. "Rankin is really dangerous."

"In case you've forgotten . . ." Signy pulled me to my feet, ". . . so am I."

CHAPTER 12

"MY GODS," MAJA WHISPERED. "The whole city is burning."

She wasn't wrong. She, Viggo and I had flown Signy and Ondyr into the capital, bringing the crystal with us and leaving Finna and Jande in the relative safety of the palace. As we'd traveled, we'd been careful to avoid the hot zones—but it was impossible to miss the waves of destruction coursing below us. Flames still roared through the residential area, consuming the town-homes that had once housed our government officials, and sending plumes of black smoke billowing into the night air. We could barely see the moon through the haze, and what little patches of sky we were able to glimpse were dirtied with ash that fell like rain. The tang of charred wood assaulted my nostrils, digging sharply into my lungs and leaving me with the aware-ness that each breath was too short; too shallow; too void of oxygen.

"I can't breathe." I doubled over once we'd touched down behind the senatorial complex.

"Well, you're going to have to," Maja said sharply. "So, stand up, and let me clear you."

"Clear me? What are you—oh!"

My spine immediately stiffened as Maja waved her hand. A waterfall of light coursed through me, running from the top of my head down my throat and ending just below my belly button. I was immediately lighter, freer, and, most importantly, *able to freaking breathe.*

"Thanks." I exhaled.

Maja turned her attention to the massive structure behind her. It housed not only the senators' offices, but the meeting rooms and private storage facilities that kept confidential government records . . . including, apparently, my tracking code.

"Rankin's here," Maja announced. "He's looking for Narrik. We need to intercept them before they transfer Aura's code."

"Then we'd better get inside," Viggo said grimly. "Aura, stay between me and Signy. If anything comes at you, I want you to run."

I tightened my grip on my sword and shot him a look. "Haven't you figured out by now, I don't run from my problems?"

"Yeah." Viggo slid the hand not holding his weapon through his hair. "But I had to try."

"Running from your homicidal grandfather and the monster who drugged the queen would not make you weak," Signy offered. "Just so you know."

"I'm not running," I repeated. "Now get moving before Maja has to clear my lungs again."

Viggo shot me a look of resigned frustration, but jogged toward the back entrance. He wrenched the door open, and waved us inside. Once we were all in, he turned to Maja with a frown. "Okay. Where is he?"

Maja closed her eyes and held very still. I glanced nervously down the darkened hallway. Eerie flickers of orange light came through the windows. The fire wasn't close, but it was big enough that it dominated everything it touched—including air.

"Rankin's moving through the western corridor," Maja finally announced.

"And Narrik?" Viggo asked.

"Southern corridor—leaving the basement-level records room."

"Good. They're not together yet." Signy glanced over her shoulder. "We intercept Narrik first—once he's in custody and we have possession of the code, we use whatever communicator he has to inform Rankin of his treachery. Viggo, do you still have that trans-muted crystal?"

"I do." Viggo patted the pocket in his cargo pants.

"Excellent. We stay together, we move as a unit, and under no circumstances are we to kill Narrik. No matter how much we want to." Signy spoke the last words as if they pained her. "We need him as bait to draw Rankin back."

"And then we can kill him?" Maja didn't bat an eye.

"We'll discuss it in committee," Signy said. I wasn't sure whether she was joking or not.

"Move out," Viggo instructed. "Aura, stay—"

"I know. Stay between you and Signy." I raised my sword and followed Viggo down the hall. "Since when do you treat me like some delicate snowflake? Huh?"

"Since you became our sole regent, and the official head of Alfheim." Viggo glanced back at me as he jogged. "Queen Aura."

My stomach tightened. But I didn't have time to process Viggo's words—or my devastation at losing the woman I'd become so close to. The full weight of Constance's crown now rested solely on my head, and I could only focus on the mission: capture Narrik, retrieve my code, and convince Rankin his 'servant' had betrayed him.

One step at a time.

We reached the southern corridor in no time, and quickly descended the steps to the basement records room. What we saw made my blood run cold.

"You." I raised my sword at the sight of Fyrs Narrik, in his tattered, military regalia, standing beside a glistening fountain. Instead of water, the fount spouted golden holographic tickets, each of which bore the likeness of one of Alfheim's key governmental personnel. Narrik spun around to face me, a shimmering ticket in hand and a shocked look on his haggard face.

"By order of the queen, you are hereby commanded to turn yourself over for questioning regarding the abduction of Alfheim's esteemed *Opprør*, and the drugging of our regent, Queen Constance." Signy raised her sword and stepped forward. "And I suggest you put that code ticket back. *Now.*"

Narrik's eyes darted from Signy to Viggo to Maja to Ondyr, before finally settling on me. "What code ticket? Yours, *Princess Aura?*"

"It's *Queen Aura* now." I stepped forward so my sword was level with my aunt's. "And you heard her. It's over, Narrik."

"And what exactly do you think is over?" Narrik's menacing voice echoed off the stacks of records. "I have your code. I can track you from here to eternity. But more importantly, the dark elf who's hunted you all from the moment you were born can finally claim you as his rightful property."

"Aura is nobody's property." Viggo's sword glinted, its threatening silvery blue blade sparking as he fell in line with Signy and me. "We'll ask one last time. And then we'll have to kill you."

"I'd like to see you try," Narrik growled.

"So be it." Maja launched herself at Narrik. She moved in a blur of wings and fury, striking him from the side and forcing the code ticket from his hand. It fluttered gently to the ground, a stark contrast to the thud with which Narrik hit the side of the fountain. I scrambled to pick the ticket up, shoving it into my cargos before joining Maja in her assault.

Narrik had scrambled to his feet, and was using the dagger he must have carried on his belt to deflect Maja's energetic shots. Silver light pinged off the blade as it reflected blows from my furious friend. While Maja delivered her energetic attack, Viggo and I mounted a physical one. We moved to opposite sides of the aisle that surrounded the fountain, and crept closer to our enemy. Narrik, distracted by Maja's unrelenting assault, didn't see us coming until we were close enough to strike. Viggo leapt forward, driving his sword into the flesh between Narrik's ribs. The monster's cry set my teeth on edge, but I held my focus and struck from the other side, slicing clear through Narrik's shoulder.

"Arugh!" Our enemy turned, sending a spray of blood arcing across the stone floor. He staggered forward, swinging at me with his good arm. As I jumped back, Signy charged him from behind. Narrik must have caught sight of her reflection in my sword, because he halted his attack on me, squatting low to the ground and striking out with his leg as he spun around. The move caught Signy off guard, and she threw herself to the right, somersaulting across the stones to avoid being struck. After a rotation she leapt neatly to her feet, and charged. Narrik was ready for her, lashing out with a roundhouse that forced her back again.

"He's not going to make this easy," Signy shouted. "Aura, shield me and Viggo while we go in!"

I didn't stop to question her. Keeping my sword raised, I dropped my energy to the ground and reached out until I felt the protection I always carried around me. With a breath I pushed it outward, straining its balloon-like confines until it slipped over Signy and Viggo. Then I opened myself up to the darkness, letting the energetic swarm merge with the brilliant, white light I drew up through my feet. Once I'd formed my signature blend, I sent it through my balloon, charging its edges with a toxic, silvery light.

"Fools," Narrik shouted. He raced toward Viggo, delivering a fierce front-kick that would have left my boyfriend staggering back. But I sent a surge through my protection, and the minute Narrik made contact he shrieked in pain. The dark blend had done its job.

"Who's the fool now?" Viggo swung his sword. Narrik rolled out of the way, then jumped to his feet and threw a right hook at Signy. The protection burned his fist, which sizzled at the hostile contact. He let out a howl, clutching his hand to his chest and whipping his head back and forth like a cornered dog.

"You're wasting your time," Narrik warned. "Rankin is coming. And when he does, he'll kill every last one of—"

Thwap!

Narrik's words turned to a gasp as Ondyr's arrow struck him in the ribs. He doubled over, clutching his chest as a pool of blood dribbled onto the ground. Maja quickly flew in, pulling Narrik's arms behind his back and binding them together with a rope that looked like it possessed at least a basic level of magic. Narrik strained against the hold, but with his rapidly diminishing blood supply, he was no match for the *älva* . . . or her bindings.

"Keep him alive," I ordered Maja. "We want Rankin to believe he defected."

"If I have to." Maja knelt down and extracted the arrow. Narrik shrieked as a fresh wave of pain coursed through him, but Maja ignored the noise and whipped an elixir out of the satchel she wore on her waist. She quickly poured it over the wound, which smoked angrily before knitting itself closed. When Narrik whimpered, she leaned in and pressed her forearm to his neck. "If you make so much as one wrong move, I'm reopening the hell out of that. And you *will* die. Are we clear?"

Narrik nodded feebly. He was probably too exhausted from the massive blood loss to do anything more. But just in case, I ripped a piece of fabric from the hem of my tank top, and tied it across his mouth. Then I lifted my sword so the tip dug lightly into the fabric of his shirt.

"Also, if you say a word I'll drive this sword straight through your chest. And unlike that arrowhead, the Dual Sword *doesn't* have a magical remedy. Are *we* clear?"

Narrik's defeated head slump served as my confirmation.

"Access his com," Viggo ordered. "There's got to be a way to reach Rankin through that."

Narrik's eyes widened, whether in fear or anger, I couldn't tell. But when Ondyr marched forward and stripped the communicator off Narrik's wrist, he didn't try to fight back. He merely watched in resignation as

Ondyr manipulated the device until an image of Rankin popped up.

"Excellent."

Ondyr tapped the hologram. It emitted a high-pitched buzzing. A few seconds later, Rankin's face filled the space above the com. Anger radiated from his knitted brows and thinly set lips as he barked, "Where are you? You were supposed to meet me at the back stairs."

"Your 'servant' isn't going to be able to meet you." Ondyr held the communicator directly in front of his face. "Why don't you talk to me, instead?"

"Ondyr?" The *V* between Rankin's brows deepened. "Where the hell have you been, son? Your mother has been worried sick."

"I highly doubt that," Ondyr said. "And that's not your concern. What you should be worried about is the fact that your so-called spy is a double agent. He's been working with Alfheim this entire time."

"Oh, has he?" Rankin didn't look convinced.

"He just handed Aura Svartalfheim's protection stone—the one thing she'd need to deactivate the castle's barrier, and come in and kill the entire top layer of government." Ondyr panned the communicator over to me. While he'd been talking, I'd removed Narrik's gag, and pulled Finna and Jande's fake stone out of my pocket. Now I held it in my palm, and tilted my head to the floundering Narrik.

"Need any more proof?" I asked.

"I—she—they're lying, sir!" Narrik spluttered. "I

would never go back on our word. You know my loyalty lies with Svartalfheim—not this wretched hovel I was forced to endure for so long."

Rankin's eyes narrowed. "If they're lying, how did they get our stone?"

"That's not our stone! They've made it all up! It's a knockoff; a replica that doesn't even—"

"Silence!" Rankin held up one hand. He closed his eyes, adopting an expression I'd seen on Maja dozens of times. He was scanning. Narrik continued to plead, but after half a minute Rankin opened his eyes.

"It's a match," he glowered. "You've given them our greatest protection. How dare you?"

"No! Please, I would never—"

"You are dead to me." Fire danced from Rankin's eyes. "If I ever catch you on my realm again, I'll rip you apart and feed you to the firewyrms."

"But you need me," Narrik pled. "I procured the princess' trace for you."

"And where is that trace? Mmm?"

"I—it's . . ." Narrik's chin dropped to his chest.

"Exactly. But no matter—I no longer have need of you. While I was waiting, one of my more *competent* servants delivered exactly what I needed to convince my wayward granddaughter to come home once and for all."

"I'm never joining you," I vowed.

"Oh, but you are." Rankin's cruel laughter filled the room. "And when you do, you'll finally fulfill your prophesy and drive the realms to war. *Daughter of Svar-talfheim.*"

"Where is he now?" Viggo growled. "I swear to Frigga, I will drive this sword straight through the hole where his heart should be."

"Ah, but then you wouldn't get to see your friend before she dies." Rankin steepled his fingertips together. "Pity. I heard you had *such* fun getting to know her on your visit last week. That unicorn ride . . . I understand it was *quite* the event."

Panic gripped my gut and I whirled to face Viggo. "Oh, gods. He has Idris."

"Meet me at the top of Alfheim's tallest waterfall." Rankin's lips thinned into a smile. "Alone. Unarmed. And ready to surrender. You have twenty-four hours until your friend dies."

"No," I whispered.

Rankin's smile deepened. "Long live the queen."

CHAPTER 13

"**Y**OU'RE NOT GOING ANYWHERE, young lady." Signy stared me down with the mom-glare I'd learned to loathe. It had kept me from sneaking out *too often* in high school, and no doubt she hoped it would keep me from traipsing after my homicidal grandfather now.

"I don't really have a choice." I glanced up at Viggo. "Do I?"

"Hell if I know." He raked his fingers through his hair. "But I'm with your aunt—I don't want you anywhere near the guy."

"I don't want me anywhere near the guy either." I threw my hands up. "But what am I supposed to do? I can't let Idris die!"

"Nobody is dying today." Maja spoke authoritatively from the end of the table.

"So you have a plan?" I asked hopefully.

"Well, no . . ."

I dropped my arms and rested my forehead on the back of my hand. "Great."

After Rankin's announcement, we'd sent Narrik off with a team of royal guards. They were instructed to hold him in a dungeon I hadn't previously known existed—a dank, holding cell located in the basement of the senatorial complex. We'd deal with him later . . . after we figured out how to keep both me and Idris alive. Now, Viggo, Signy, Maja, Jande, Ondyr and I were gathered in the regent's office on the third floor of the senate building. The wall-sized window provided a devastating view of the fires still ravaging the capital. They'd diminished since our arrival, but our emergency crews were only so big. It would take a miracle—or an unexpected summer storm—to douse the blaze before daylight.

"We obviously can't let Aura go to Rankin." Ondyr played with the string of his bow, which he'd slung behind his chair. "And we can't let Idris die. Which leaves us with . . ."

"Not a lot of options," Viggo finished.

"And not a lot of manpower," Signy added. "I just spoke with Larkin—most of our warriors are still fighting off the intruders. Svartalfheim breached *en masse,* and there's no way we can keep our citizens safe if we divert a team to the waterfall."

"How did they open that many portals?" I asked. "We had protections in place."

"True. But they had an insider familiar with our

systems. And worse, familiar with the way our operatives think. We changed our protocols, but Narrik knew enough to find a workaround that hacked our altered systems." Signy shook her head. "He screwed us over big time."

I rolled my head to the side. "So, what do we do?"

"We wait for reinforcements," Viggo said. "Maja, where are we on our backup?"

Maja glanced at her com. "My dad's on his way. It'll take a few hours, but he's bringing half the faerie corps with him. The rest are remaining behind to protect the colony in case there's an attack."

I blinked. "When did you call him?"

"When the queen fell," she said grimly. "I had a feeling things were going to get worse."

"Thanks," I whispered.

She shrugged. "That's what friends do."

I sat up. "Are you saying we're friends now?"

Maja's eye roll was her only answer.

"Think, team," Viggo urged. "How do we get Idris away from Rankin? And Rankin away from Alfheim?"

"Can we use *älva* dust to extract the Crown Princess?" Ondyr asked. "It got you guys into the palace —maybe it can get her out of wherever Rankin's holding her?"

"Maybe." Maja tilted her head. "I'd have to be with her for the extraction, so if Rankin's keeping her with him it won't work. But if she's being held somewhere else . . ."

Viggo nodded at Ondyr. "Have the warriors send

you an aerial scan of the waterfall, and work with Maja to get an exact location on both Idris and Rankin."

"On it." Ondyr tapped his wrist device. He pulled up a holo-screen, which he shared with Maja.

"Professor Bergen, you and I need to figure out a way to distract Rankin long enough to cover Idris' extraction." Viggo leaned forward. "Maybe if we—"

"Rankin's with Idris," Maja interjected.

Four heads turned as one.

"He's holding her here—in the open, on top of the waterfall." Maja expanded the hologram atop Ondyr's wrist, then pushed it forward so it hovered over the center of the table. "See those two signatures at the base of the cypress trees? One's bound, gagged, and clearly in distress—that's Idris. The other is emitting unnaturally high levels of . . . can dark elves feel *glee?*"

"That's not good." Ondyr turned to Viggo. "What's plan B"

"There is no plan B." My hands balled into fists. "If he's that close to Idris, there's no way Maja can dust her out. Rankin would kill them both before Maja even touched down."

"There has to be another way," Signy said firmly. "What if—"

"Signy," I said quietly. "I have to go. Idris' realm needs her."

"And your realm needs you," Viggo growled. "You're not risking your life. Not on my watch."

"What if she doesn't risk her life?" Maja's wings

fluttered behind her. "What if we could protect Aura—set up a blocker Rankin couldn't penetrate, no matter how hard he tried?"

Viggo's brows furrowed in suspicion, but I leaned forward. "Go on."

"After everything that went down last year, my mother and I started working on a new kind of protection—one rooted deeper in dark magic than anything we've worked with before. We modeled it off the clearing columns we used to break the cells that were holding the senators, but reverse-engineered the energy."

"Meaning?" Ondyr asked.

"Meaning we double down on darkness, halve the light, and throw in a hit of *älva* dust to . . . um . . ." Maja glanced at me. ". . . to control the minds of whomever we use it on. Sorry, Aura. We got the idea from what Narrik did to your grandmother."

"That's kind of brilliant," I admitted. "Using their own ideas against them."

"Would that work on Rankin, though?" Viggo asked. "If he's the dark mage everyone says he is, won't he be immune to the dust?"

"Nobody's immune to the dust." Maja tossed her braid over her shoulder. "Especially if we're hitting them with an unprecedented level of magic at the same time. It'll work. Trust me."

"But if it doesn't . . ." Viggo trailed off.

"It will work," I said. My gut didn't doubt it one bit.

"I can enhance Maja's protection from the inside. And since it's me he'll be focused on, I'll know if Rankin's about to strike—or if he's overcoming the dust's effects for any reason."

"I don't like it," Viggo said.

"I know." I placed my hand on his arm. "But you've got to trust me—this is our best shot at saving Idris. And, if we're lucky, at defeating Rankin."

"Professor Bergen?" Viggo turned to my aunt. "What do you think?"

"I think Alfheim's queen should not put herself in danger." Signy's stern expression conveyed her disappointment. "But . . ."

"But," I urged.

"But I respect your loyalty to your friend." Her eyes softened. "And I appreciate you wanting to be a different kind of leader than your predecessor."

"So . . . you have faith that Maja can get this done?"

"I have faith that Maja *and* Sirra can," Signy corrected. "I presume your mother is coming with the war party?"

"She is," Maja confirmed.

"And I presume you've successfully conjured this protection before? Preferably in another high-stakes situation?"

Maja just stared at Signy.

"I see." My aunt folded her hands together. "Maja, I'll ask you this one time. Are you absolutely certain you can protect my Aura?"

"If I wasn't, I wouldn't ask you to trust me with her life," Maja swore.

Signy nodded. "Then let's map out our plan. But if *anyone* thinks of *any other way* we can do this . . ."

I swallowed the fear that nudged at my gut. *This will work. It has to work.* We were going to save Idris. We were going to destroy Rankin. Because if we didn't . . . if Rankin made my dark prophesy come true . . .

The realms would be driven to war. And it would all be my fault.

"Hey, Sorenssön. You have a minute?" I bumped Viggo's shoulder with mine.

"What's up?" He didn't take his eyes off the smart board where he and Ondyr were sketching out an extraction strategy. They'd identified Rankin's weakest points, and were determining attack positions for the incoming *älva*.

I stood on tiptoe to whisper in his ear. "I need to talk to you. Alone."

Viggo finally looked at me. If he noticed the anxiety in my eyes or the tension in my hands, he didn't out me. He just turned to Ondyr and said easily, "I'll be right back. Keep working on this, okay?"

Ondyr tapped a spot on the bottom right of the board, adding an *älva* to the growing formation. "On it."

I slipped my hand through Viggo's and pulled him toward the door. "I'll be quick. I promise."

"Take your time," Ondyr called. "I'm better at this than he is anyway."

"Keep telling yourself that!" Viggo countered.

Despite my nerves, I couldn't help but laugh.

I led Viggo into the sitting room adjacent to the conference room. The queen had an entire suite in this wing, and since that title fell squarely on me now . . .

I closed the door and pressed my back to its wood. Then I took a deep breath and turned to Viggo. "Listen, I just wanted to say—"

"I still don't like this." Viggo crossed his arms. He looked down at me with a glower so intense, it would have intimidated the fiercest dark realm warrior. But I knew Viggo too well. Underneath his anger pulsed a massive dose of fear—one I couldn't help but share, though I'd commandeered mine into a much more compact dose.

"I need you to do me a favor." I wrapped my arms around my chest and held tight. "If for some reason this doesn't go the way we hope it does—"

"So help me Frigga, if you're about to say what I think you are—"

"Just listen." I squeezed my ribs. "If this doesn't go well—if Rankin captures me, and forces me to do what the darker part of my prophesy says I'm fated to do—"

"You're *fated* to lead the realms to peace from here. With me," Viggo vowed. "I won't let Rankin change that."

"If he does," I continued as if Viggo hadn't spoken, "I need you to look after Alfheim in my place. Be her fiercest protector. Be both the *Verge* and the leader she'll need to survive the darkness, and bring back the light."

"Aura." Viggo's voice wavered over my name. "If there's any part of you that thinks this isn't going to work you have to tell me."

"My gut says it will work," I said. And it did. "But there's always the chance something could go wrong. And if it does . . . then I need to know that Alfheim will be okay without me."

"Stop." The word was fierce, but Viggo's eyes were pleading. "I can't go there."

"Well, I need you to go there." I forced my arms from my chest, and reached out to grasp Viggo's hands in my own. "If I'm taken, and the dark realms believe Alfheim is vulnerable, they won't hesitate to swoop in. They'll power down the Alfheim Tree, they'll force the *älva* back into camps, they'll use their dust to control Midgard, and they'll convert all of our light into darkness until the cosmos is pure chaos. They'll enslave our citizens, and make their lives a thousand times worse than they were under Narrik. If I'm taken, our world—and all the worlds—stand to suffer more than you and I could possibly imagine. And if that happens"—I drew a shaky breath—"then I need you to step up and be the leader Alfheim needs."

Viggo pressed his lips together. His eye twitched. Was he fighting back tears?

"Promise me," I urged him. "Please."

"I will *always* protect Alfheim." Viggo's voice cracked over the words. "Just as I will *always* protect you. If you're taken—and that's a big *if*, because I will fight to the death to make sure that doesn't happen—then you have my word that I'll look out for our home. But my first priority will be to get you the Helheim back. Do you understand me?"

"Your first priority has to be Alfheim," I said quietly. "If I'm a threat to it—if whatever Rankin does to me makes me a liability in any way—then you cannot come after me. What's that thing we learned in our Key class? 'The needs of the many outweigh the needs of the few?'"

"Screw Key class." Viggo squeezed my hands. "If you're putting me in charge, I make the decisions. And I will *never* decide to stop fighting for you. *Never.*" His eyes sparked, emerald fire emanating from their depths.

"Viggo, listen—"

"No, you listen, *Glitre.*" Viggo stepped closer so our chests practically touched. "From the moment I met you, you've ignored me and infuriated me and overall been a massive pain in my butt."

"Hey!"

"You have. When you caught me talking to Ondyr in the woods, and I told you not to get involved—you ignored me. When I swore I'd kick your butt in our *Verge* final—you upped your game just enough to beat me. Barely."

"I crushed you on that exam," I corrected.

"Keep telling yourself that." Viggo shrugged. "Watching you learn that dark stuff with Maja last year nearly destroyed me. And now—seeing you walk into this situation? It's killing me, Aura. Nobody in their right mind would be okay watching the girl they love risk their life like this. It's insanity."

My body stilled as my pulse thundered in my ears.

Viggo loves me? My eyes locked on his. "Wh-what did you say?"

"I said this is insanity. And I know you have to do this, that you'd never let your friends suffer beca—"

"No. Right before that."

Viggo's brow furrowed in concentration. "That you're killing me?"

I bit down on my bottom lip. "Did you say you . . . *love me?*" The last two words came on a whisper.

"Well, yeah." Viggo tilted his head. "I thought you knew that."

"You've never said it," I whispered.

"Isn't it obvious? We've been together for a year and a half. We train together, we've had each other's backs in every life-or-death fight we've been through—which is entirely too many, considering we haven't even graduated yet. We work together, I'm your plus-one at all state functions, and whenever either of us has a problem, we turn to the other for help first. Plus we have these marks on our wings." Viggo reached up to tweak the tip of mine, and a shiver of pleasure vibrated down the appendage. "And we make out. A lot. I thought you knew."

"Yeah," I breathed. "But you've never *said* it."

"Ah. Well, in that case . . ." Viggo's dimple popped. "Aura Nilssen, I love you. I love your generous heart, and the way you'd do anything for your citizens. I love your stubborn mind, and the way you refuse to yield to me ever, in anything, no matter how much sense it might make to admit I'm right."

"When you're right, I—"

"Shh." Viggo placed his finger to my lips. "I love the way you stand up for what you believe in, regardless of what anyone else is going to think, and no matter how steep the personal cost. And I love the fierce loyalty you show to your friends. I love that spark inside of you, and even though it pushes me to the brink of insanity, it also pushes me to be the very best version of myself I can possibly be. You bring that out in everyone you meet—making the world a better place, one inspiration at a time. You shine like nobody else I've ever met—that's why you're my *Glitre*. And that's why, whatever happens today, I *will* be right at your side. We're a team—now, and always. Because . . ." Viggo shifted his finger so it crooked beneath my chin. He pressed gently upward and dipped his own head until my lips were nearly level with his. "I love you."

Breath whooshed from my chest at the declaration. Viggo Sorenssön loved me. *Me.* A half dark elf with a price on her head and a realm to rule. A girl who'd somehow managed to drag her friends down a road from which we might not emerge. Somehow, in spite of all my mistakes, all my shortcomings, and all my liabilities, he loved me anyway. And I . . .

My eyes met Viggo's in a moment of absolute clarity. "I love you, too," I whispered. "I think I always have. Even when you were driving me nuts back in our third year with your—"

Viggo's lips stopped my words. All coherent thoughts flew out of my mind as he pressed his mouth to mine and kissed me as if he might never stop. His hands reached up to grasp my hair, his fingers tangling in the fine, blond strands. I pressed myself closer to him, the heat searing from his body into mine. Warmth blossomed in my chest, and a pulse shot from my heart due south. Its slow burn sent my hands on a downward trajectory, and I pressed my palms to the small of Viggo's back and pulled his hips against mine. A low groan escaped his lips, the vibration sending a fresh wave of emotion coursing through me. I mentally eyeballed the couch. What would happen if I dragged Viggo over to it, ripped off the tank top that was obstructing my view of his *exquisite* chest, and just went for it alrea—

"Oh! So *that's* what's keeping you guys." Elin's voice pulled me out of my lusty fog. "Don't mind us; we're just trying to stop the end of the world in the other room."

Mortification doused me like a firehose. I tried to step away from Viggo, but he slid his hands from my hair to my back and held me close.

"We'll be there in a minute," he said calmly. "We were just finishing up."

"Mmm." Elin's eyes slid from Viggo's hands to his hips. "Well, don't be too thorough. Signy's right on the other side of that door."

"Shut up, Elin!" Fireballs flamed my cheeks.

One corner of Elin's mouth turned up in a smile as she backed slowly toward the exit. "I just meant you might want to be a little more discreet. Or, you know, wait until your aunt *isn't*, like, fifteen feet away."

"Goodbye, Elin," Viggo said pointedly.

My bestie snickered all the way into the other room.

When the door clicked closed behind her, I raised my head and met Viggo's amused grin. "I guess we'd better go help them."

"We will." Viggo bent down to give me one more languid kiss. My insides pooled into a puddle of pure hormones. When he finally pulled away, I had to lean into him to remain standing. "You okay?"

"Great," I squeaked. "Never better."

"Me too." Viggo rested his forehead against mine. "I'm glad we cleared the air."

"You and me both," I murmured.

We stood there for a moment, just holding onto each other in what might well be our last moment of peace. Viggo's heart pounded against my chest, whether coming down from our kiss or gearing up for our fight, I didn't yet know.

I slipped my hands up so my palms rested lightly

against Viggo's chest. Then I lifted my chin and looked at him questioningly. "So, we're good?"

"We're always good." His dimple popped again. "Ready to save Idris?"

I nodded. "And destroy my grandfather."

It was time to get back to work.

CHAPTER 14

THE FOREST WAS DARK as I crept toward the waterfall. High winds had delayed the faeries' arrival, so it was nearing dawn when Maja's parents and their warrior backup reached the capital. Once there, Maja and her mother, Sirra, took a small protection unit and headed straight to the waterfall to scout the best location from which to work their unusual style of magic. Her father, Rafe, stayed behind. He and his ground captain huddled with Viggo, Ondyr and Signy, going over our plan until it was indelibly ingrained in each of their heads. There was no room for error on this mission. And if we failed . . .

Don't think about it. Just focus on the job.

I snaked my hand around Viggo's as we approached the edge of the forest. This was our stopping point. Rafe had used *älva* dust to cloak him along with the rest of the airborne team, and they'd be keeping watch from the cypress range on the mountain adjacent to the waterfall. The ground unit, led by Signy and Ondyr, was to hide in the cave looping behind the fall's spout, emerging only after Rankin was debilitated. And I was to fly in solo, fully exposed, without my beloved Dual Sword to keep me safe. The only protections I had were my powers, my friends, and whatever dark magic Maja and her mom were conjuring at that very moment. *No big deal.*

"Stay safe." Viggo took my sword from my hand. He now held one in each of his, double-fisting the Dual Swords that were forged from the same metal as Thor's hammer, Mjölnir, and had protected Alfheim for centuries. *Double NBD.*

"You too." I reached up to tighten my ponytail. Then I checked that the laces of my combat boots were secure. Distractions were the last thing I needed. Plus, doing something so mundane soothed my mind.

"Remember, if anything goes wrong I'll extract you before you can say, 'Go to Helheim, Rankin.'"

"Good to know." My eyes met Viggo's in a worried stare. "Look out for Signy. And Ondyr. And Rafe. And, well . . . all of them."

Viggo's gaze softened. "You've got this, *Glitre.*"

With a tight nod, I stood on tiptoe to kiss his cheek. Then I turned toward the mountain, bent my knees, and launched myself into the air. "I'll see you on the other side," I called down.

"We'll be ready," he vowed.

Gods, I hoped he was right.

I didn't look back as I flew to my waiting point on a

rocky outcrop halfway up the hill. The ground unit was already in place in their mountain-top cave. The airborne team was positioned behind the wall of cypress trees. Once Viggo was in place, I would make my move.

And hope I wasn't signing my own death warrant.

After a few minutes, my com glowed softly. Viggo was in position. It was go time.

Breathe, Aura. You've got this.

Gulp.

Before I could chicken out, I stood on my toes, took to the sky, and followed the sound of rushing water. As I swung around the mountain, the wind blasted me with a damp spray. Icy drops coated my torso, and I pulled back before I got completely soaked. Redirecting myself, I flapped hard, fighting against the breeze as I halved the distance between me and the mountaintop. With a final burst of power I reached the ledge, careful to stay clear of the mist whipping off the stream. The wind had thrown me off-course, and I ran the rest of the way to my mark. Maja and Sirra could only protect me for as long as I stayed in their range. And with Rankin being so powerful, I didn't want to leave a single thing to chance.

Not when so many lives were on the line.

I'm set. I projected the thought to my dark faerie friend. I knew she'd heard me when I felt the tingle of a familiar energy slip around my bubble. It carried Maja's resonance, but with a slight edge. This protection was heavy—marred with a darkness unlike the ones we'd used in the past. Something sinister snapped around its edges, forming tiny sparks along the outside of my space. I had no doubt it would deflect whatever Rankin threw at it. The only question was, how long would it last? Hopefully, we'd only need a few minutes to extract Idris and take Rankin down, but could I manage to last that long? And, for that matter, could my friends?

Whatever you're doing, knock it off. The voice that filled my head wasn't mine. I froze, terror locking my body down as I realized someone had managed to hack my brain. If it was Rankin, I was totally screwed.

Relax. It's just me—Maja. I exhaled in relief as I recognized my friend's familiar, sarcastic edge.

Oh my gods, how are you doing this? I released my shoulders from where they'd taken up residence beside my ears.

It's part of the protection. Keep walking; you look suspicious, Maja sent.

Right.

I dragged one foot, then the other, toward the cypress Rankin had indicated as our meeting point. He was nowhere to be seen, which meant he was probably lurking out of view, just waiting to ambush me. I forced myself to stare straight ahead—I didn't want to give away the position of my backup.

You're doing great, Maja assured me. *He doesn't know where they are—though he suspects someone's here. He's not stupid, just evil.*

Truth, I sent back.

Now, blend up your dark/light swirl. Hurry—he's on the move.

My breathing quickened, and I hastily drew a dose of light up from the earth. I let it fill my body, then opened myself to its opposite. I'd always felt the energy as a swarm of angry bees, and this time was no different. They descended on me in droves, pouring into the tiny hole I created in my protection as if I were the last flower in the patch. Whether their intensity was due to the proximity of a truly evil presence, or whether it was because they sensed my desperation, I couldn't tell. I only knew that this time when I blended them with the tiny white lights swirling inside of me, the merge burned in a way it never had before. My body felt as if it was filled with live wires, each popping and sparking like a downed power line in a storm. Either I was mounting the defense of my life, or

. . .

You're not dying. I could practically hear Maja's eye roll. *It's a perfectly normal enhancement given the wrap my mother and I have around you.*

A heads-up would have been nice, I grumbled.

Suck it up, Princess.

Don't call me that!

Sorry. Maja chuckled. *Queen.*

Ugh. *Just do your job.*

He's moving.

At Maja's warning, I pulled my shoulders back. Every nerve in my body pinged to life as I stirred the double helix inside and drew its silver energy into my palms. If Rankin made a move, I would blast him all the way to Helheim.

If he didn't kill me first.

Lose the negativity, Maja ordered. *He's fifty yards away, at your five o'clock. All teams are in place. Make your move.*

I slowly turned around, so my back was to the waterfall's ledge. As predicted, my grandfather walked slowly across the mountaintop. The wind whipped his silvery-white ponytail across his neck, and he casually brushed it away. He wore the same long, silver tunic as before, only this time his sleeves were marred with dirt. Idris must have put up a fight when he'd taken her. Hopefully she still had some scrappiness left. If the fury in his eyes was any indication, we were going to need every possible advantage we could get.

"I told you to come unarmed." Rankin's words dripped with hatred.

"Do you see any weapons?" I challenged.

"I feel yours," he countered. "Drop your protections, granddaughter. *Now.*"

"It's *Your Majesty,*" I corrected. "And that wasn't part of our deal."

"I told you to come alone and unarmed." Now he was thirty yards away.

Bring him closer, Maja urged.

How? I sent back.

Just keep him talking.

"I am alone." My calm voice stood in marked contrast to the panic rising in my gut. Every fiber of my being was revolting at being this close to Rankin. The sensation was made worse by the frenetic buzzing of the swarm inside my chest. *Down, bees.*

"And unarmed?" As predicted, Rankin kept walking. Now he was just twenty yards away. "Drop your shield, Aura."

"Not until you hand over Idris," I challenged. "That was our deal."

"And I never go back on my word." Rankin snapped his fingers and my friend appeared at his side. Panic burst from my chest at the sight of Vanaheim's crown princess bound by thick, black cords, and gagged with what looked to be a dark magic-laced cloth. Her head lolled listlessly against her chest, and her eyes were firmly closed—whether because she'd passed out, or because she didn't want to see the monster in front of her, I couldn't tell. The only thing I knew for sure was that my friend was in trouble. And I was the only one who could help her.

"Hand her over," I demanded.

"Drop your shield," Rankin countered.

I narrowed my eyes. "You first."

A low chuckle came from Rankin's throat. The sound of it set my teeth on edge. "You have fight, granddaughter. I'll give you that."

"Give. Me. My. Friend," I growled.

"Fine." Rankin waved his hand lazily. "But you should know, I've placed a sleep lock on her."

"What the Helheim is a sleep lock?"

"A curse," he said calmly. "One only I can lift. One

wrong move on your part, and . . ." Rankin mimed slitting his throat.

Skit.

We'll deal with that later, Maja pressed. *Just get her away from him.*

But his magic is—

I SAID NOW.

My breath hitched at the roar inside my head. Stretching out my arm, I shot a beam of silver light from my palm. As it snaked around Idris' waist, I wrenched my hand back. Rankin's eyes widened as Idris launched across the mountaintop, easily covering the twenty yards that separated us in the time it took me to release a breath. She landed beside me with a heavy thud, her body folding on top of itself in an uncomfortable-looking ball.

"I kept my part of the bargain," Rankin said calmly. "And now—"

He broke off as a blinding beam of light shot up from the ground. It surrounded me and Idris, encasing us in a thick, white tube.

We're pulling Idris. Stay where you are! Maja ordered.

Her order was moot. The energy coming off whatever surrounded me overwhelmed my senses to the point where I couldn't move, couldn't see; I could barely *think.* Everything was white—pure, blinding, brilliant white. For one blissful moment, I was encased in light.

And then Rankin attacked.

CHAPTER 15

THE DARK ELF LASHED out. A thick, black bolt slammed into the tube just as Idris and I began to lift upward. The motion halted whatever Maja and her mom were doing, and I landed on my backside with a heavy *thwack.* Ignoring the pain that jolted up my spine, I scrambled to my feet and grabbed Idris by the hips. Since she was still unconscious, I was able to maneuver her without resistance. Before Rankin could strike again, I bent my knees and spread my wings.

Extract us again, I ordered Maja. *I'm going to fly us out.*

He's locked in on you, Maja warned. *I won't be able to pull you both.*

Then take Idris. I didn't hesitate. *I'll take care of myself.*

But that means—

DO IT!

A second bolt rammed into the tube, and I sent one final thought to Maja.

NOW!

Light surged through the tunnel. *It's go time.* I bent my knees, tightened my grip on the crown princess, and pushed every ounce of strength I had into launching her into the air like a Midgardian cheer-leader. Maja's pull was already drawing Idris upward, and with my additional boost, my friend moved swiftly up the near-blinding tube. She sailed higher, passing quickly through the white tunnel before abruptly disappearing. Maja must have placed some kind of portal at the end, because one minute I had a clear view of Idris rotating higher, and the next she was just gone.

She's okay? I asked.

We have her, Maja responded. *Is there any way you can follow her up?*

I don't think so. But I'll try.

I bent my knees and tried to jump, but my feet were stuck firmly to the dirt. Spreading my wings, I tried to lift myself with my *other* appendages, but they weren't strong enough to break whatever hold Rankin had on me. I was trapped—for the moment, at least. And if I didn't think fast, this wind-blown ledge was going to be my grave.

Think, Aura . . . I bit down on my bottom lip as a third bolt rammed the tube. Then a fourth. Rankin was doubling down on his attack. He clearly was a master of darkness—but then, he'd had a lifetime to conquer skills I'd only just begun to learn. I wasn't going to overpower him—not even with Maja and Sirra fighting him with me. The only way I could beat Rankin . . .

That's it! I pushed the thought at Maja. *We let him in —let him take control of me.*

Are you insane?

Probably. But it's the only way we're going to overpower him. We have to use his own power against him.

I think you inhaled too much älva *dust.* I could practically hear Maja's snark. *There's no universe in which allowing Rankin any kind of control over you is at all a good idea.*

A fifth jolt rocked the tube, forming a massive crack in its white surface. I stumbled as the crack deepened, wrapping all the way around my casing and breaking it clear in half. The tube that had protected me from my grandfather dissipated, melting into a cloud of fog before blinking out of existence as if it had never been there at all.

Oh, gods.

Blast him, Maja urged. *It will give you enough time to run and—*

Her words fell silent as a thick, black smoke coiled like a snake around my feet. It wound its way up my legs, constricting as it moved and holding me firmly in place. It continued up my body, squeezing my chest in its vise-like grip, and I gulped down air as if I were drowning. For all I knew, I was. I had no idea what Rankin had planned, but I knew I needed to stay alive long enough to figure out how to survive.

Please, gods, let me survive.

I sucked down one last gulp of air before the smoke-snake circled my neck. Only seconds had passed, but already the edges of my vision were going dark. The pressure on my windpipe was pushing me to the edge of consciousness. Through the fog, I made out the shadowy figure of my grandfather marching toward me. And behind him . . . no. They couldn't be that stupid. We'd seen what Rankin did to Constance—it would be a suicide mission to get anywhere near him. And the faeries were smarter than that.

Weren't they?

A white beam lit the sky. It struck the ground with a thunderous *boom*, rattling the snake loose. I drew a generous breath, orienting myself just in time to see Rankin raise a hand behind him. Without looking back, he shot a black beam from his palm. It struck the faerie who'd been brave enough to come after me, singeing his wing and sending him spiraling downward. Another white beam rocketed downward, this one followed by a pair of *älva*. Rankin downed them as quickly as he had the first. His lips curved up in a cruel smile as he sent an additional bolt into the cypress grove where the remaining members of the airborne unit were perched. They scattered, taking to the skies as the bolt ignited the grove where they'd been just seconds before.

Fly. I pushed the thought into the air, hoping Maja could still hear me. *Tell your dad and Viggo to get the hell out of here before—oh, gods!*

Rankin's hand was raised. His fingers curled inward as he pulled me closer. Only ten yards separated us now, and being this close to such an intense level of darkness sent my stomach roiling. I wanted to lash out; to fire silvery beams into the hole where his heart should have been. But I wasn't strong enough to kill him. None of us were. And fighting him off was only going to get us all hurt. Or worse.

The only way to defeat Rankin was to surrender.

The *älva* were regrouping over Rankin's shoulder. Whether he sensed them or not, I couldn't tell. But the moment I spotted the familiar, silver wings of the guy who'd owned my heart since that first infuriating, "Hey, *Glitre*," in the dining hall, I knew I didn't have a choice. I focused on the buzzing swarm inside of me, projected it outward, and locked myself within a dome of darkness.

I was trapped with Rankin, encased within a coliseum of my own making. Only instead of lions, I faced off against a monster. And instead of cheering spectators, I was surrounded by a friend-family who'd been willing to give their lives to save mine. I sensed Viggo's panic somewhere outside the dome—his fear for my safety somehow channeling through the shared mark on our wings, and burying itself deep within my heart. But I knew what I was doing.

I hope.

With a breath, I dropped my shoulders and shook my hands at my sides. The power buzzed within me, firing up and down my torso like a series of detonations. As Rankin moved closer, I drew it down my arms, loading my palms and waiting for just the right moment.

Rankin was going to die.

"I must say, I am impressed." He took another step forward. The darkness surrounding him weighed me down, pressing against my chest in a way that made breathing nearly impossible. "You conjured a dark dome all on your own. You *do* have potential, don't you, granddaughter?"

Instead of responding, I re-opened the hole in my bubble—the one I used to draw darkness in. I held myself perfectly still as I willed the swarm inside of me to invite their friends—specifically, the ones pouring off of Rankin in an infinite stream of horror. They were only too willing to comply, firing at me in a jet of pure evil. Pain rocked my nerves as they poured into my body. The light in my chest was all but doused as a weight I'd never experienced pressed down on my heart. I was drowning—being suffocated by the very thing I'd invited in. But I knew it was the only way. Rankin was too powerful for any light being to defeat. Which meant that, at least for now, I had to go dark.

Even if it hurt like a mother.

A fresh wave of fear jolted my wing, and I knew Viggo was trying to break through to help me. But I couldn't look at him, couldn't let Rankin know that at that very moment, a half-dozen *älva* were gathered just outside the dome, fighting to get in. Their white beams bounced right off the bubble, silenced by the cloak I'd created around Rankin and me. Soon enough, I could drop the barrier . . . and I'd need them to be ready when I did. But things were about to get messy. And I couldn't have their blood on my hands.

A shudder wracked my spine as I drew one final hit on Rankin's energy. Then I uncurled my fists, lifted my palms, and let the sparks course through me.

The release was nearly euphoric.

Pain mixed with pleasure as a stream of dark, grey light burst from my hands. It struck Rankin in the chest, launching him off the ground so he slammed against the barrier I'd placed around us. The *älva* dove, lighting the sky up with bolts that dissipated the moment they hit the blockade.

Too soon, I pressed.

Rankin picked himself up, rage igniting his soulless eyes. "If that's how you want to do things . . ."

I squared my shoulders and released another surge. This one hit him in his shoulder, spinning him around so his back was to me. I'd learned enough at the academy to know a strike to his third energy center would seriously weaken him, not to mention deliver a blow to his confidence. Narrowing my eyes, I directed my next attack to the center of his back. This time, instead of pushing him down, my beam struck lightly then retreated. As I called it back to me, I drew more of Rankin's power, more of his darkness. My body absorbed it like a sponge, quickly melding it with the light in my chest until a new, more intense blend coursed through me. I sent an offensive strike at

Rankin's base center, thrilling when he dropped to his knees. But without warning, he flung a hand up. A black bolt jarred my chest, and I stumbled backward, clutching at what felt like a massive hole right over my heart. I fired off a retaliatory beam, then pulled another hit-and-draw on Rankin's third center. When I was fully charged up, I raised both hands and struck with everything I had.

Rankin crumbled to the ground. His limbs shook and his face scrunched in a look of clear agony. But even as he convulsed, he slowly pushed himself upward. He wasn't giving up. In fact, he was getting stronger—somehow drawing strength from the charges I'd thought would kill him. My plan wasn't working.

And I didn't know what else to do.

"Is that all you have? Hmm?" Rankin's eyes had turned almost completely black. He staggered toward me, limping like a creature out of a horror movie. "Because if you're truly to drive the realms to war, you're going to need to deliver more than that. This, maybe."

Rankin curled his fingers and I was wrenched from the ground. My feet kicked the air as something thick wrapped around my throat. My hands flew to my neck, but I clawed at nothing. My chest seized and breathing grew impossible, the airflow blocked by an invisible cord that refused to yield.

"Or this, perhaps."

A fierce stabbing pierced my gut. I relinquished my

hold on my neck as I fought to remove whatever blade Rankin had driven into my stomach. Although my hands closed around thin air, the stabbing continued to shoot wave after wave of agony from my skin to my spine. Was this how I was going to die?

"Or, possibly, this."

Fog clouded the edges of my vision and as I closed my eyes, I howled in agony. Every inch of my skin, from my scalp to my toes, erupted in boiling, surging, flames. I swiped desperately at my arms, fighting to extinguish the fire that was sure to consume me. But when I opened my eyes I realized the fire was in my mind. My skin remained untouched . . . though the sensations didn't let up.

"Face it, *granddaughter*. You'll never defeat me. We can continue this little game, or . . ." Rankin closed the distance between us. He reached up with one, pointed fingernail, and scraped it lightly beneath my chin. ". . . you can accept your prophesy and come willingly. I promise it will be a lot less painful."

On the last word, Rankin sent a fresh wave of fire coursing over my skin. I shrieked, no longer able to maintain any sense of control. The silvery blend inside of me flickered, then died out. This was it. This was how it was going to end. After everything Signy had taught me on Midgard, everything I'd learned at the academy, all of the drills Viggo and I had run in *Verge* training, all the work I'd done with Maja . . . all of it had been for nothing. I'd been too weak to overpower the one being whose darkness could drive the entire cosmos to war . . . so long as I was at his side.

As the pain overtook me, and blackness colored my vision, I closed my eyes and sent one final thought to everyone who'd put their faith in me.

I'm sorry.

CHAPTER 16

I HEARD THE BATTLE before I saw it. It raged around me, electrified *zaps* and hisses blasting through the air, lighting up the night even behind my closed eyelids. I blinked them open, immediately regretting my decision as my brain was assaulted with a strobe-like series of flashes. Something swooped out of the sky, diving low and delivering what looked to be a lightning bolt into the ground. The earth trembled, rocking me where I lay in a tight ball. My arms released their hold on my knees, and I pressed my palms to the dirt, pushing myself into a seated position. All around me, winged warriors threw bolts of white light, dive-bombed a shadowy figure huddled beneath a filmy, black shield, and drove glowing, arm-length swords into the translucent bubble that surrounded him. The warriors were fierce, but their opponent appeared unharmed. How was a single being outmaneuvering an entire army?

My spine stiffened and I sat upright with a jolt. This was no ordinary being. This was Rankin, master dark mage, lead senator of Svartalfheim, and the man intent on using me to destroy the realms. This was a battle we stood very little chance of winning. But losing wasn't an option.

It never had been.

The world spun around me as I pushed myself to my feet. *Everything hurts!* I stumbled backward, steadying myself on the trunk of a nearby cypress. It was thick, and sturdy, and I opened the centers in my hands to pull on its steadying strength. As I did, soft footsteps sounded from my right. I turned, fists drawn, ready to fend off whoever had come to force me into a life I most definitely *did not want.*

"Down, girl. It's only me." Viggo's familiar voice sent a waterfall of relief coursing through me. I exhaled in relief, resting my forearms on my knees as he ran to my side. When he reached me, he stood back, hesitating.

"What's wrong?" My words came on a raspy breath. My chest burned, as if a smoldering fire raged deep inside it. And my skin felt as if it had just been put through a pizza oven, then deposited on the surface of the sun.

"I don't want to make it worse," Viggo said quietly. "You're . . . smoking."

Still doubled over, I glanced at my bare arm. My skin looked intact, but sure enough, a faint mist rose from its surface. It reminded me of a mountain stream on a frosty day, when the heat of the water gently rose to form a pearlescent fog. Only instead of white, this fog was black. And instead of delivering peace, the mist sent me into a full-on panic.

"It's *him*." I scrambled backward, swatting at my arms. "I let his energy inside me, thinking I could overpower him by becoming him. But it didn't work, and now—"

Viggo closed the distance between us, placing his hands on my arms and making my panic surge harder.

"Don't touch me!" I screamed. "It might infect you, too, and—"

"Aura, look at me." Viggo's voice was commanding. Controlled. He wrapped firm hands around my shoulders, and lowered his head so our eyes were level. "You're not going to infect me, but you do need to help me. We're getting destroyed out there."

He jutted his head over his shoulder just as Rankin fired a black bolt at an oncoming *älva*. The faerie was thrown off course, and sent spiraling into the trunk of a nearby tree. She crumbled to the ground in a heap, her body bent at an unnatural angle.

Oh, gods.

"Tell me what to do." I swiped at my arms again, trying not to freak out at the thin layer of smoke still rising from my skin.

"Take one of these." Viggo released my shoulders. He reached for his waist and drew one of the Dual Swords from his sheath. I reached for its hilt, but quickly withdrew my hand.

"What if this . . . stuff"—I waved my hand in front of my body—"—inside of me hurts it?"

Viggo shrugged. "We'll do what we always do. We'll figure it out. Together."

My insides warmed, and a fresh surge of black steam rose from my skin. I tried not to shudder as I was enveloped in a murky fog. Viggo reached for his waist, grabbed hold of his own sword and drew it from its sheath. It glowed a light blue before sending a charge at my sword. They'd done this before—hit each other with some sort of energetic high-five—so it wasn't completely foreign. But this time, the charge traveled up my arm, pinging through my torso before settling around my heart. Heat radiated through me, pushing against my ribcage as if someone had turned on a slow-cooker in my chest. My eyes widened as the temperature increased, and I reached out to grasp Viggo's hand as a surge of steam radiated from my body. The air was immediately filled with the stench of sulfur, and I tried not to gag as the black fog rolled over me. But a second later the stench—and the steam —were gone. My skin had ceased smoking, and I was left feeling as close to normal as a girl could, after her magic sword had cleansed her grandpa's dark energy from her body.

Oh my gods, my life.

"Whoa." Viggo squeezed my hand. "You okay?"

"Never better." I groaned as I righted myself. Releasing Viggo's hand, I swung my sword in a light circle and assessed the mountaintop battlefield. "Where are we needed?"

"That's my *Glitre*." Viggo grinned. "Rafe's team are hitting Rankin from all sides, but he's got himself barricaded inside that shield. You said that energetic protections don't work against physical attacks, right?"

"In most cases," I corrected. "But this guy's got a whole other level of crazy going on."

"Agreed." Viggo narrowed his eyes. "My best guess is that if we coordinate with the air and ground teams —let them drive him back while we ambush him from the sides—we stand the greatest chance of success."

"And if you're wrong?"

Viggo shrugged. "We go down fighting."

"Viggo!"

"I'm kidding. There's, like, thirty of us. And one of him. We've got this."

I nodded. We did have this. Because if we didn't . . .

No. Don't go there, Aura.

"Okay," I said. I drew my shoulders back, and tried not to freak out at the charge my sword sent through my arm. It was almost as if it was saying, *yes. We* do *got this.* "Gamma formation, on your mark."

Viggo pulled his elbows back and crouched low to the ground. "In three," he announced. "Two. One."

We launched ourselves into the air, and barreled for opposite sides of the monster hellbent on destroying us all. At some point while I'd been blacked out, Rankin had crossed the stream that fed to the waterfall's mouth. Viggo and I flew over it together, making sure to stay out of Rankin's field of ocular vision. Whether he could see us with his third eye, or whatever he had going on, was anyone's guess. Once we'd cleared the water, Viggo hooked left while I swung right. He raised his sword in the air, signaling to the aerial unit that we were going in. In the distance, Rafe pulled back, no doubt reworking whatever strategy he had in play. But I couldn't think about him just then—the gamma formation led with a heavy attack, and I needed all of my focus on my target. He stood a hundred yards away, sheltered beneath a black dome that extended just beyond his arm's reach. We'd be on top of him in half a minute, and if that thing was functioning . . .

Maja. You there? I hoped our connection was restored now that I was free of my self-imposed blocker.

Now you're talking to me? That stunt you pulled was beyond stupid. Never silence your—

Shut up and listen, I pressed. *We need to break that shield. Do you have a lock on my location?*

Do I look like this is my first battle?

Since tensions ran high, I let the sarcasm slide. *I'm going to hit him at his five o'clock. If you hit his seven, Viggo and I will both be able to slide in.*

On it. Resolve filled Maja's tone. *But you and I are going to have words when this is ov—*

Going in!

I fired a beam at Rankin's right flank. His spine straightened as my attack pierced his shield, and he quickly whirled on one heel to face me. As he did, a second beam struck his left flank—this one thicker, more forceful, and loaded with considerably more darkness. Maja was *livid.*

Let him have it, I urged.

I am. Her words came on a grunt as she sent another beam at Rankin.

Not wanting to be outdone—and also, needing to expand the hole I intended to slide through—I mirrored her attack. Rankin shifted back and forth. He must have deduced Maja's blows were more damaging than mine, since he turned to his left and raised his hand in the direction of his supposed assailant. Only, Maja was projecting her attack. Which meant that when Rankin uncurled his fingers and fired off a black bolt, it headed straight for—

"Viggo! Look out!" I shrieked as Rankin's death dagger barreled down on my boyfriend. Viggo swerved at the last second, spiraling out of harm's way before raising his sword and diving through the hole Maja had created with her beam. Knowing Rankin's focus would be on Viggo, I flapped harder and lifted my own sword. As Viggo sliced at my grandfather's ribcage, I tucked through the opening I'd bored and drove my sword into Rankin's right thigh. A fierce cry rang through the mountaintop, echoing off the trees and driving the few birds that hadn't evacuated to take flight. As Rankin's knee gave out, I wrenched myself to the right, circling back and striking again—this time, slightly higher. Blood spurted from Rankin's groin, and I swiped at the sticky liquid coating my arm as I flew out of his reach. When I circled back again, Rankin lay on his side. The dirt beneath him was stained with red, and though he'd obviously lost a lot of blood, he hadn't given up his fight. He'd managed to reseal his barrier. Viggo continued to strike from behind, but his sword couldn't pierce the shield. If Rankin gathered enough strength to strike again . . .

We had to end this. *Now.*

Send in the aerial unit, I ordered Maja. *You and I can create the opening they need. If we hold it, it should give them enough time to debilitate him. And you saw what our swords can do.*

Dad's on his way, Maja confirmed. *Hit him at your twelve o'clock. If I do the same, it'll create a bigger hole.*

On it.

I signaled to Viggo, who was slashing furiously at Rankin's shield. Our eyes locked, and I jabbed my thumb over my shoulder before flying away and taking cover behind one of the large cypress trees. When I turned back around, Viggo had retreated just enough so I could strike. On Maja's command, I fired off another shot. It hit Rankin from behind, creating a fresh hole in his barrier. As he turned his shoulders, Maja's beam merged with mine. It bored into the protection, widening it just enough that Rankin's entire back was now exposed. I continued my assault, and a wave of momentum pulled my attention upward. The *älva* were attacking, descending on Rankin with swords and daggers and one particularly intimidating mace. They barreled toward their target, keeping his focus forward while Viggo flew around his back. For the first time, I noticed that our ground team was with them. They ran below the faeries, helping the fallen and driving Rankin back. Ondyr fired off shots from his bow, one of which slipped through a tiny opening in Rankin's shield to bury itself with a swift *thwap* inside his shoulder. Signy ran alongside him, her sword drawn, while the rest of their team charged close behind.

It was now or never.

My arms trembled as I threw a fresh surge at Rankin. Every muscle in my body ached, and though I'd been giving everything I had, I knew I had to draw strength from somewhere . . . anywhere. A hundred percent just wasn't enough.

More, Maja urged.

I'm. Gasp! *Trying!*

I sucked in a breath as I sent another surge. It erupted from my hand, an electrified wave barreling through my palm and striking Rankin in the spine. Maja's beam joined with mine, intensifying the vibrations wracking my arms. My hands shook, and my aim was unsteady as I shoved one final surge at the monster on the ground. His back arched as his barrier split in two, cracking along the center and crumbling to the dirt.

"Attack!" Signy led the charge. She and Ondyr came at Rankin from the front, while the *älva* descended from the air. Maja and I maintained our assault, our beams now surrounding Rankin and holding him in place. And with his attention firmly focused on the wall of assailants coming from all sides . . .

Slurp!

Rankin never saw Viggo coming. Never saw the Dual Sword glow a fiery blue as it lifted over his head. Never noticed the silent rage pouring off the *Verge* who'd spent his life running from Rankin's tyranny—who'd lost his parents on this monster's orders. Despite all his protections, his dark magic and his curses, he failed to notice the man on the mountaintop who was poised to take him down.

And that failure cost him everything.

Viggo's sword bore straight downward, piercing the delicate skin at the base of Rankin's neck, and driving past his vertebrae in the direction of his heart. Viggo didn't hold back; he didn't stop until the hilt of his blade was nestled firmly against Rankin's shoulder. The world ground to a halt as Viggo adjusted his grip, placed his boot atop Rankin's rib cage, and twisted the sword. With a grunt he pulled it out at an angle, leaving a massive hole that bubbled with blood. It poured freely down Rankin's back, the sight sending my stomach into a full-on churn. Rankin wavered, swaying back and forth twice before landing face down in the dirt.

I tentatively reached out, searching for the now-familiar darkness I'd let into my space. But the only signatures I sensed on the mountaintop were benevolent—Signy's fierce love, Ondyr's determined defense, Rafe, Maja and Sirra's unyielding loyalty, and, standing atop the corpse of the man who'd raised my father, was the guy who'd do anything to protect both me and our realm. Viggo turned slowly, raising one fist to signal for the attack party to stop. And as our eyes locked, I knew in no uncertain terms that this act of our nightmare had closed. Rankin was dead.

It was over.

I lowered my hand, held tight to my sword, and *finally* let myself breathe.

CHAPTER 17

RANKIN'S BODY WAS TRANSPORTED to the capital. We didn't know how deep dark magic ran, and we weren't taking any chances sending it back to his family. He would be cremated, and his ashes locked in the royal vault where *nobody* could get them.

Once Rankin's corpse was on the move, the aerial team flew to the main part of the city. There, they assisted with the roundup of the dark elves, and helped the ground teams close down the remaining portals. It was another several hours before the city was secure, and my friends and I spent that time helping in the shelter that had been set up in the academy's great hall. Maja and Sirra joined us, the two of them using their abilities to heal as many wounds as they could—both physical, and mental. Ondyr and Signy showed up after they'd debriefed the warriors, but Viggo had skipped their meeting. In fact, he'd refused to leave my side. He claimed that as *Verge* Key and co-minister of defense, it was his duty to protect the queen. But the panic hadn't quite left his eyes, and I sensed his proximity was as much for his peace of mind as it was my own. *Not that I'm complaining.*

Sunlight crested over the academy's towers by the time all of the evacuees were finally settled in their makeshift cots. When the great hall was calm, I slipped out a side door and typed on my com.

Meet me in our conference room in five minutes? -Aura

Then I walked down the quiet hallway, my sheathed sword sitting listlessly against my hip. It hadn't lit up since the waterfall, and I sensed it was flat-out exhausted.

Same, sword.

When I entered the conference room, I dropped into my usual seat at the big oval table, and rested my head against the high back of my chair. Every part of my body felt heavy, from my legs to my arms to my soul . . . to my eyelids . . .

The shuffle of footsteps jarred me from my nap.

"She's asleep. Let's come back later," Elin hissed.

"She wouldn't have commed us if it wasn't important." Finna sounded uncertain. "Right?"

"It's okay, guys." I rubbed at my eyes. "I'm up."

"That's your fault." Jande turned to Ondyr with a frown. "I told you to walk quieter."

"I did tiptoes like you said!" Ondyr objected.

"Seriously. It's fine. I shouldn't have nodded off anyway." A massive yawn parted my lips, and I covered my mouth with my hand. "Sit. Everybody."

A sheepish-looking crew took their places around the table.

"What's this about?" Maja asked. "Has there been another attack? If the faeries missed a portal, we can get them to—"

"Everything's fine," I assured her. "Well, as fine as it can be, considering. Is Idris all right?"

"After I extracted her, I removed Rankin's curse. It was some heavy duty dark magic, by the way—took everything I had to get it out." Maja shuddered. "Then I scanned her and sent her back to Vanaheim. She's emotionally scarred, but physically okay. Her parents send gratitude for her safe return, and want you to know they'll be in touch once everything's settled down."

"Good." I nodded. "Now that that's settled, I called you here for two reasons. First, I want to say thank you." I leaned forward and studied the faces of the team around me. "Each and every one of you risked your lives to protect our realm. Finna and Jande, you guys coded the crystal that helped us take Narrik into custody. What we're going to do with him, I honestly do not know. But he'd still be out there, colluding with undesirables to take Alfheim down, if it wasn't for the two of you. Our realm owes you a great debt."

"It owes us nothing." Finna waved her hand, at the same time as Jande blurted, "I want a troll diamond! I want to travel to the future to see how *fabulously* rich and happy I am."

"You're not happy now?" Ondyr arched a brow.

"Obviously, I'm happy with *you*." Jande patted his boyfriend's hand. "But I know even more awesomeness is coming. And I want to see it."

"No troll diamonds," I said firmly. "Time travel's an issue for another day—or no day at all."

Though it would be cool to see the future . . . or the past. Those Midgardian Vikings always fascinated me. I wonder . . .

"Fine," Jande huffed. "I'll take my 'great debt' payment in the form of *other* crystals, then."

"It was a figure of speech." I chuckled. "I just meant, thanks. A lot."

Jande unleashed an award-winning sigh.

"Elin." I faced my best friend. "You kept things together from the ground. Signy told me you were in constant communication between the teams, and that they knew their positions because of you. Thank you."

Elin nodded. "Least I could do."

"Ondyr," I continued, "you and Signy charged straight into battle, no questions asked. You had our backs, and made sure the *älva* were never in more danger than they had to be. You're a rock star, and I'm glad you're my family."

"Same, cuz," Ondyr said with a grin.

"Maja." I turned my attention to the girl currently inspecting her fingernails. Maja hated attention almost as much as Jande hated missing out on a cartload of crystals. But it had to be done.

"Say nothing. That's thanks enough for me."

"Well, it's not for me." I leaned forward. "You and

your mom protected me in ways nobody else could. If it wasn't for you, Rankin would have taken me out the moment I set foot on that waterfall. I owe you my life."

"What you owe me . . ." Maja narrowed her eyes. ". . . is to never do anything so stupid as shutting me out in the middle of a battle again. What the Helheim were you thinking?"

"I was thinking if he managed to get in my head, he could get to you, too." I raised my hands. "It's not an excuse. But I was so scared that I wouldn't be strong enough to protect all of you that I did the only thing I could think of. I locked you out. It was stupid, and I won't do it again. Promise."

Maja crossed her arms. "Fine."

"I'd also like you to *please* consider staying on full-time, as a member of my cabinet. But that's a big ask, and we can talk about it tomorrow."

"I'll do it," Maja said quickly.

My brows shot to my hairline.

"A week ago I would have said no, but you guys clearly need me."

"We really do," I said.

"And if you're going to rule this realm all by your-self, you're hardly in a position to cloak it, and monitor it, and make sure all those bloody portals stay shut, too. With their help, of course." Maja jutted her chin toward Viggo and Ondyr.

"You'll do all of that?" I asked hopefully. "From this cabinet?"

"I'm going to have to." Maja shrugged.

I jumped up from my seat.

"If you hug me, the deal's off," Maja warned.

I reluctantly sat back down.

"Welcome to the team," Viggo said.

My gaze shifted to the guy who'd slain my metaphorical dragon. Viggo had shoved his sword down the spine of the man who'd killed my parents, colluded with Narrik, and spearheaded a horrific attack on Alfheim. And, most importantly, he'd had my back at every single terrifying turn.

"And Viggo." My eyes softened. "Thank you. For everything."

"I've got you, *Glitre*," he said simply. "Always will."

I had no doubt that he would.

"You said you wanted to talk to us about *two* things," Finna said cautiously.

"I did, and I do." I nodded. "As you know, the queen is dead. She was murdered by Rankin just hours ago. We'll need to arrange for a state funeral, alert the leaders of the light realms, and follow whatever protocols Eunice has in place for a transition of power."

"I'm so sorry, Aura." Finna's kind eyes sought mine across the table. "I know things weren't always easy between you, and I'm sure you wish you'd had more time together."

"I do," I admitted. "I also wish I had more time to learn this job. I only found out I was in line for the throne just under two years ago. I am nowhere near prepared to take it on solo."

"We'll help you," Elin promised. "We'll read all the

briefings Eunice has, and break them down into cheat sheets like we used to do at Granite High."

Finna stared at me with incredulous eyes. "You guys cheated?"

"It's an expression," Elin explained. "We made short little lists of the most important facts to memorize, and quizzed each other on them. We didn't actually cheat on tests."

"We left that to Britney." I rolled my eyes.

"Speaking of, who knew she'd actually turn out to be useful?" Elin shook her head. "Don't get me wrong, she's still Bitch Face. But that tip about Narrik was good intel. Maybe she's redeemable after all."

"I wouldn't hold my breath," I said drily. "Speaking of Narrik, we need to locate and extract his family. If anyone on Svartalfheim gets wind of Narrik being an alleged traitor, they'll be on a hit list, for sure. And it's not their fault their patriarch's a monster. So . . ."

"I'll go," Ondyr volunteered. "I'm familiar with the realm, and should be able to get it done quickly. So long as I can take a protection team—no way am I getting stuck there ever again."

"I'll have one assigned to you," Viggo promised. "Professor Bergen is familiar with the warriors; she'll be able to recommend the best unit. We'll be in and out before you know it."

"We?" Ondyr frowned.

"I know how bad it was for you there," Viggo said quietly. "I wouldn't make you go through that by yourself."

Gratitude bloomed in Ondyr's eyes. "Thanks, man."

"No worries."

I folded my hands together. "That just leaves us with this whole power transition. I'm not going to lie—it kind of freaks me out. Without a skilled leader, Alfheim's more vulnerable than ever. We're going to need to make sure our defenses are airtight, and our alliances as strong as they can be. We'll need to host Nidavellir, and lock things down with Vanaheim, and consider sourcing an, uh, enlightened representative of Midgard who can motivate their people to stand with a realm they don't know exists, and—"

"Aura." Viggo reached over to rest his hand atop mine. "We've got this. First of all, you're not unskilled. You've ushered in an era of unity *despite* everything Constance did to subvert that very goal. May she rest in peace," he added hastily.

"It's okay," I assured him. "She was far from *perfekt*. None of us are. We have to work with the hands we're dealt."

"Well, the hand you were dealt is *us*," Elin assured me. "And we're here to help. And so are the senior cabinet members—they've been through all of this before. Not a transition, maybe, but they know a hell of a lot more about ruling a realm than we do. They're on your team too, and I know they'll do everything in their power to help us out."

"Thank gods." I exhaled.

"As for alliances, I'd say you've got the one with Vanaheim wrapped up pretty tight," Maja offered.

"That message I got from the king and queen was loaded with gratitude. You saved their daughter—I'd wager they'll do anything you ask from now 'til forever."

"*We* saved their daughter," I corrected. "And it was our fault she was taken in the first place. Rankin only abducted her to get me to do what he wanted."

"Not true," Maja said. "His defenses were down enough at one point that I could scan him. He'd been moving on Vanaheim for a while. Its light is second only to ours, and he thought if he could make a base there, he could drain it for its power."

I frowned. "But he wanted me so I could fulfill that stupid prophesy."

"True," Maja agreed. "And he would have come for you, regardless. But he didn't care which light realm he made his new home. Theirs or ours—either would have accomplished his goal."

"Huh." I shook my head. *Who knew?*

"Hold on." Viggo rubbed the back of my hand with his thumb. "I thought you said the goal of the Vanaheim specter was aligned with Dragen's. You told us it had a similar energetic resonance. Right?"

"I did," Maja confirmed. "And Rankin's goal *did* align with Dragen's. Both wanted to control Aura—albeit they wanted different outcomes, but control was their mutual goal."

Recognition dawned. "So, Rankin *was* the specter, which means Dragen's still safe on Helheim."

"Safe as he can be, locked away with Hel." Elin shuddered. "We still owe Wynter one for that."

"We do," I agreed. "Once she and the other fourth-year *Bridgers* are released from their relocated retreat, I'll check in with her about destroying Rankin's remains, too. She may have heard something while she was in the Cloak, and I want to make sure *nobody*, dead or alive, does anything to help whatever passed for his soul."

"Sounds right up Wynter's alley," Elin agreed. Her com beeped, and she glanced down. "It's Signy. She says we'll begin transition protocol tomorrow."

I glanced at the clock on the wall. *Five minutes past eight a.m. . . .* "What are we supposed to do for the rest of the day?"

Viggo squeezed my hand. "It's been a hell of a night. And I'd wager tomorrow's going to be a long one, too. The best thing we can do right now is sleep."

He didn't have to ask me twice. But even so . . .

"We'll jump in tomorrow," Elin assured me. "Cheat sheets, light realm outreach—all of it. We promise."

I glanced around the table, taking in the lined eyes and drawn faces of each of my friends. "You guys go," I decided. "There's one thing I have to do first."

"You need sleep too," Finna said softly.

"I just want to talk to Viggo. Then I'll be right up," I assured her. "Promise."

Our meeting ended after that. Maja, Finna and Elin shuffled wearily toward our dorm, while Jande and Ondyr headed to the Great Hall to pick up a snack before turning in. When it was just Viggo and I left in the conference room, I took his hand and led him to the window. We stood there in silence, staring at the orangey glow of the smoky sky.

After a while, Viggo shifted beside me. "What's up, *Glitre*?"

"You had my back through every horrific turn." I slipped my other hand into his, and tilted my chin up to meet his eyes. "You've been my rock through all of this—the good, the bad, the downright terrifying."

Viggo shrugged. "That's what training partners do."

"Not like this," I said quietly. "When I first met you, I disliked you on sight. And it took a *long* time for you to grow on me. When I saw these marks . . ." I glanced at the sword stamped on the tip of his wing, ". . . and I realized what the Norns intended for us, I could not have been more horrified."

"You're really selling the moment," Viggo said drily.

"Let me finish." I pressed my lips together. "But every time you've had the chance to disappoint me—to turn tail and run, to pick the easy path over the greater good—you've chosen to step up. You've taken on more than anyone could have asked of you—and certainly more than I have any right to expect from you. You've been my partner in every sense of the word. Which is why, someday *way* in the future . . ." My chest shuddered as I drew a slow breath.

"You okay?" Viggo asked gently.

Just nervous. So very nervous.

But I pulled my shoulders back, and pressed

forward. "Which is why, someday *way, way, way* in the future . . ."

"I get the timeline." Viggo's dimple popped.

"I want you to be my King. Not King Consort, like tradition dictates. But full-on King. Co-ruler of Alfheim, and my equal in every way."

I held Viggo's gaze as my words landed. His eyes widened, surprise painting his *perfekt* features as he registered what I was asking. "Are you sure?"

"Absolutely," I vowed. "I couldn't have done any of this without you. Well, I could have, but it would have sucked big time. And I don't want to keep doing it on my own forever. You're a good leader, and you love our realm—possibly more than anyone I've ever met. Your willingness to put your life on the line for her over and over again proves that. She deserves *two* rulers with her best interests in heart. And someday, when we're *way* older, and ready to make that kind of commitment . . ."

Viggo quirked one brow. "You saying you want to marry me, *Glitre*?"

"No!" I blurted. "I mean, not now. Someday, maybe. If it's what *we* decide. Together. Without the Norns."

Viggo chuckled. "Those mate marks never had anything to do with my decision to be with you. You know that, right?"

"I do," I assured him. "But I need this to keep feeling normal. Or, as normal as it can, considering I'm about to be the queen and you're my minister of defense, and neither of us has even graduated yet."

"It's a strange life we live." Viggo pulled me into his

chest. His arms slipped around the small of my back, and he rubbed slow circles with his thumbs as he said, "And to answer your question, yes. I'll be your king. So long as you call me Your Majesty."

"Dream on." I rested my cheek against Viggo's chest.

We stood like that, holding each other as morning dawned across a smoky Alfheim. It would take time, and a lot of rebuilding, but one day she would shine again. And until then, I was secure in the knowledge that I was surrounded by the best possible team, wrapped in the arms of the best possible partner, and in the best possible position to bring Alfheim into a new era of peace.

CHAPTER 18

"YOU READY?" TEARS GLISTENED in Signy's eyes as she fluffed out the train of my over-the-top coronation gown. It was long, and blue, and bore an inordinate number of sparkles across its tightly fitted chest.

In the month that had passed since our battle with Rankin, I'd been too distracted by my crash courses in How To Rule A Realm, and Forging Alliances 101, to notice what my royal seamstress had been up to. Or how many sequins she'd squirreled away. *Sigh.*

"Oh, just look at you!" Signy's sniffles echoed throughout the throne room.

"You can't be crying already," I protested. "We're just taking the portraits. The ceremony doesn't even start for another half hour!"

"I thought your graduation was rough—I went through two handkerchiefs by the time the ceremony was over." Signy dabbed at the corner of her eye. "But this . . . oh, my sweet girl, it's too much. I raised you, and today you're becoming queen. You'd better get used to the tears—there will be plenty more."

Signy adjusted the angle of my crown. I'd only ever worn one in my entire life—the blue flowery one I'd donned for the state dinner when I'd first met Idris. That night might as well have been decades ago.

Today's crown was considerably larger. It had the same blue, flower-shaped crystals as its "informal" counterpart, but its fleur-de-lis peaks were easily three inches tall, and it was forged from a metal that looked suspiciously similar to my sword. I hadn't bothered to ask about its origin. If I was wearing a mini-Mjölnir on my head, I would freak out. Either that, or I'd raise it high and shout, "For Asgard!" just to see if I, too, could summon thunder.

Maybe after the coronation . . .

"There." Signy stepped back to admire her handi-work. "You're *perfekt*. And I don't just mean your looks. You are, and always have been, absolutely wonderful, from brilliant brain to front-kick-delivering toe. You know that, don't you?"

A small smile tugged at my lips. "I love you, too."

Signy's eyes glimmered as a fresh wave of tears threatened to overflow.

"No more crying," I admonished her.

"It's just . . ." She blinked rapidly. "Your mother would have loved this moment. She'd know just the right words to guide you into the next stage of your life. She always knew how to put everyone around her at ease. And she would have been so incredibly proud of all you've accomplished, and all you've agreed to take on."

"She'd be proud of you too," I said quietly. "You've been one badass proxy parent."

"Language," Signy chastised.

"I'm the queen," I said cheekily. "Remember?"

"Titles carry no weight with me." Signy didn't crack a smile.

"Fine," I sighed. "You've been one heck of a proxy parent. Better?"

"Much." Signy's gaze swept up and down my body. "Hair, crown, gown—everything looks to be in . . . Aura?"

"Mmm?"

Signy's eyes narrowed. "Show me your shoes."

Heat crept up my neck as I sheepishly lifted the hem of my gown.

"You cannot wear combat boots to your own coronation!"

"Why not?" I raised my chin, trying for a near *perfekt* imitation of my predecessor. "As regent of Alfheim, I set the tone for the sensibilities of its residents. And, as such, it behooves me to show my fellow Alfheimians that we must all be prepared to stand up for ourselves—our individual selves, our friends, and the greater good of the realm. My choice in footwear is a symbolic stance for the independence of all who wish to—"

"Oh, fine." Signy sighed in exasperation. "Clearly, I've prepared you as an orator."

"And as a *Verge*." I grinned. "As queen, I'll have to balance both worlds. I'm just trying to be prepared."

"Are you, now?" Signy ran a hand through her cropped pixie cut. "I noticed you wore heels to your grandmother's funeral."

"Yeah, well . . . it's what she would have wanted. So . . ." I shrugged.

As per Alfheimian tradition, Queen Constance had lain in state for two days. A stream of visitors had made the pilgrimage to the royal residence, and I'd stood reverently in the waiting area to greet every single one of them. My feet had been killing me by the time we'd finally held her funeral service, but I knew Constance would have been mortified if I'd worn my personal footwear of choice.

"Aura?" The door cracked open, and a timid head poked around its edge.

"Come in, Wynter." I waved my friend inside. She'd proven invaluable to our team, taking charge of Rankin's disposal, and setting up a task force of *Bridgers* to monitor the Cloak for the next few months. The five of them would make sure nobody on either side of the veil did anything to bring him back.

Now, Wynter stepped shyly into the room. "He's here."

"Who's here?" As a *Bridger*, Wynter could communicate with spirits. Her statement could have meant anyone from Jande to the late King Leon.

"Bob," she said. "He was discharged from the *Dyr* unit this morning, and you asked me to bring him."

"Right! Thank you!" In all the craziness, I'd nearly forgotten this was Bob's first day of freedom. "How's he feeling?"

"He's thrilled to be free." Wynter shook her head. "I've never seen anyone complain so much about being kept in such a beautiful facility."

"It was the 'being kept' part he took issue with," I offered. "Bob had free rein of the forest back on Midgard. He was none too thrilled to be confined to a care facility—even a five-star one."

"So he told me. All the way over here," Wynter said drily. "He's sitting in our row, so you'll see him at the ceremony."

"I can't wait," I said honestly. "Give him a hug for me."

Wynter shot me a look that communicated her lack of interest in hugging the prickly feline.

Fair enough.

"If you've got one more minute, I have a message from your dad," Wynter offered. "It's for you too, Professor Bergen, if you'd like to hear it."

Signy's spine stiffened. "Kegoth is here?"

"No," Wynter said. "He's not allowed outside of the Cloak. But I spoke with him there this morning, and he wanted me to tell you how proud he is of you, Aura. He says that he and your mother are watching over you today, and that they know you'll be a brilliant leader. You already are."

My chest tightened, and the tears I'd just teased Signy about welled up in my eyes.

"Thank you," I whispered.

"And Professor Bergen." Wynter turned to my aunt. "He and Lilly want to thank you for getting Aura safely to this day. He says you've looked after their greatest treasure, and for that they will be eternally grateful."

Signy's tears flowed freely. "Tell them I love them both. Even Kegoth, though we never met."

"He knows," Wynter said with a smile.

"Are they together then?" I asked. "Did Dad finally go to Valhalla?"

"He will after today," Wynter said. "With Rankin dead, and you surrounded by protectors—including the bobcat he selected for you—he's free to join your mother."

"Poor Bob's back on guard duty?" I frowned. "I wonder how he feels about that."

"He's thrilled to be useful again," Wynter assured me. "Though you're going to want to make sure his new living situation is more spacious than the one I just 'sprung him out of.' His words."

"Of course they are." I laughed. "I guess my first act as regent will be to install a massive bobcat playground in the forest behind the palace."

"I'm sure the caretakers will love that." Signy groaned.

"I have to go," Wynter said. "Zara's holding my seat, but the chapel's filling up, and you know how aggressive she gets when people are in her personal space."

"Tell her I said hi." I grinned as Wynter slipped from the room.

The door had barely clicked closed when another knock sounded.

"Come in," I called.

"Portrait time!" Vendya burst into the throne room, a balding man close on her heels. "The queen will stand here"—she pointed—"and should be lit up from *here*." She pointed again. "That should place the dress—and Her Majesty—in their most flattering lights. You have three minutes to set up."

The man staggered beneath the weight of the lights, stool, and camera he carried. I reached out to help him, and he shot me a grateful grin.

"Take your time," I assured him. "They can't start this thing without me, right?"

"I suppose not." Relief coated his wrinkled forehead, and he got to work.

Another knock made me glance at Signy. "We expecting anyone else?"

"It's just me." Viggo poked his head around the door. His waves had been gelled to inky black perfection, and his emerald eyes crinkled around the edges as he glanced between Vendya and the photographer. "Just wanted to see if you guys needed anything."

"Maybe some company," I said lightly. "Come on in."

"I will but . . ." Viggo checked his com. "I'm also here to tell you everyone's in place. You ready?"

"Not in the slightest. But then, what else is new?"

Viggo chuckled as he slipped through the door,

clicking it closed behind him. He crossed the room, his eyes lighting up as he took in my too-fancy gown, ridiculously ornate crown, and the smattering of braids I'd allowed to be woven into my hair. His dimple popped, and I couldn't help but drool a little at the snug fit of his blue and ivory coronation suit. With its epilates at the shoulders, and the sash across his chest, he looked every bit the fairytale prince I'd never imagined myself ending up with. And yet, here we were. Standing on the precipice of an unbelievable adventure, neither of us remotely prepared to walk the path ahead.

Here goes nothing.

An eternity passed while I waited behind the chapel's thick golden doors. Signy and Viggo had already taken their seats, and Vendya had fluffed my train one more time before scurrying through a side door to admire her handiwork from a spot in the back row. It was just me standing behind the doors, waiting to walk down the long aisle in front of a room full of dignitaries and a handful of friends, and officially become queen.

No pressure.

The blast of horns made me jump, and I quickly smoothed the front of the bedazzled princess gown—correction, *queen* gown—that Vendya had called her "crowning glor-eee!" The fanfare picked up its tempo, before trilling into a rapid-fire sequence. As the final note wavered, I pulled my shoulders back and took a deep breath. *I'm on.*

The golden doors parted, and a hundred immaculately dressed guests trained curious eyes on me. I fought the instinct to fidget, or squirm, or straight up *flee*, and forced myself to stand ramrod straight as the horns trilled again. I recognized the notes as my *go* cue, which sent another surge of adrenaline coursing through me. Tradition mandated a formal coronation ceremony, and though I was much more of a "sign a set of papers and get it over with already" kind of girl, I knew the realm deserved this experience—especially given everything it had been through for the past seventeen years. And so, instead of thinking about the kings, queens, senators, dignitaries, and "special guests" currently triggering my flight reflex, I squeezed my shoulder blades together, forced a dignified smile on my face, and took my first step.

Ninety-nine. Ninety-eight. Ninety-seven. We'd marked this over and over in rehearsals. I knew that when I got to fifty, I'd be halfway to my mark. At seventeen, I'd draw level with Viggo and Signy. And at one, I'd be standing in front of Illuminara, Alfheim's Supreme Being of Light. She had overseen coronations, state funerals, and other official functions since my great grandparents' rule. I had no idea how old she was— Eunice had been mortified when I'd asked her to find out—but whatever she was drinking/eating/taking in her morning tea, it was some good stuff. Illuminara didn't look a day over forty.

Seventy. Sixty-nine. Sixty-eight.

Keeping my eyes mostly forward, I sized up the chapel in my peripheral vision. Garlands of greenery hung from the pews, with sprays of white flowers clustered at regular intervals. Late afternoon sunlight streamed from the stained-glass windows, bathing the chapel in a peaceful pink glow. The royal florists had spent the better part of the week stringing bunches of fragrant white blooms from the windows' ledges, and as I cleared the first half of my walk I drew a deep, soothing breath. It was a mark of how far my meditation skills had come that I didn't miss a step when I locked eyes with Britney. I'd invited the least agreeable of the Keys to attend to avoid creating any further discord between us. We'd never be besties, but she was still a Key—and I didn't want any bad juju in the realm I was striving to build.

Twenty-five. Twenty-four.

"Purr..."

Bob purred his approval as I came even with my friends' row. His ears flickered, and I couldn't help but grin at his familiar, furry face. My gaze moved down the row, where each of my friends stood, decked out in Vendya-designed outfits. Jande had insisted the royal seamstress make their clothes for the big day, and he now stood proudly beside my cousin. Ondyr rocked the James Bond vibe in a navy suit that perfectly complemented Jande's ivory one. Elin, Finna and Wynter were equally gorgeous in their gowns, and Maja looked only slightly uncomfortable in her all-black pantsuit. They smiled at me, even Maja, with Elin bouncing excitedly on her toes.

"You look awesome!" she mouthed.

I responded with my most regal nod, being careful to maintain my composure. But inside, I was relieved. While everything around me seemed to be changing, I knew without a doubt our friendship never would.

Thank gods.

Nineteen. Eighteen. Seventeen. Whew.

Viggo shot me a rakish grin as I drew level with him and Signy. My aunt looked like she was about to explode with pride, and I gave another regal nod, showing her I could *totally* channel the whole queen vibe while wearing combat boots. My eyes shifted to Viggo, whose hotness factor in his Prince Charming getup was enough to make me miss a step. My cheeks pinked as I nearly stumbled, quickly catching myself and staring straight ahead for the rest of my march up the aisle.

When I reached Illuminara I channeled my inner debutante, bending my knees and curtsying low to the ground. As I rose, I my eyes were drawn to the halo of sparkles surrounding Illuminara's braided updo. They flickered in the pink filtered light, a flock of tiny fireflies dancing around the officiant's head.

Illuminara gestured for me to take my place on the padded kneelers in front of the altar. While I made my transition, she raised her arms and addressed the crowd.

"Today marks the dawning of a new era for

Alfheim. Through the ashes, our realm of light has risen. I stand before you at the will of the gods, appointed by the most holy order of seers, the Norns, and anointed by the Mother Goddess Frigga herself. It is my deepest honor to offer this blessing upon Aura Nilssen, daughter of Lilly and Kegoth, granddaughter of Constance, great-granddaughter of our most beloved Queen Silvie and King Leon. Once our crown princess, today Aura ascends as our queen. She will guide us into a time of peace and prosperity, and she will continue to demonstrate the strength of character and spirit that have endeared her to this majestic realm."

My heart thudded as Illuminara glided to the kneeler where I'd lowered myself—and my massive dress. My hands were folded in reverent prayer, and my head slightly bowed. This was it. The moment she'd say the words that would change me from Aura Nilssen, one-time Midgardian comic book nerd and current Alfheimian *Verge* graduate, to Queen Aura of Alfheim, Leader of the Light Realm and Bearer of Truth. I'd snorted the first time I'd read my full title in one of Eunice's briefings, but that was about to be my name.

No pressure at all.

A clear note rang through the church, and I raised my head to watch Illuminara sing the blessing. It was a traditional *älva* folk song—one thought to have originated shortly after the birth of the cosmos, when drops of starlight descended on Alfheim to create the faeries.

The song burst from Illuminara with the clarity of a bell, her impeccable tone captivating me enough that I momentarily forgot my nerves. I couldn't quite make out the words—old elvish was a subject I'd never been able to master. But I'd read a translation in Eunice's briefing. The officiant was blessing both me and my reign with light, and love, and abundance, and prosperity. She was channeling the Mother Goddess, and imbuing me with the wisdom of the kings and queens who came before me. I felt their presence—everyone from my great-grandparents, to Constance, to . .

Oh, my gods. Mom?

The realization that my mother was here slammed into me, knocking the breath from my chest and leaving me clutching my heart. Happiness overwhelmed me as my awareness of her presence grew. Just over the officiant's shoulder was a flicker of light that radiated pure, unadulterated love. It beamed at me with the force of a thousand suns until I was filled from head to toe with hope, and joy, and peace. My mom was here. *Here.* On my coronation day. Somehow, she'd made it all the way from Valhalla, and though I couldn't see her I knew without a doubt that she was looking right at me, beaming with pride because I'd become exactly who I was meant to be.

I love you so much. I sent the thought into the air. And though it seemed impossible, I felt a gentle light expand inside my heart. She loved me too.

The officiant finished her song, and stepped to the altar to retrieve the sacred oil. I removed my crown as she approached, placing it on the small table beside me and presenting my forehead for her blessing.

"This oil, extracted from the bark of the Alfheim Tree, channels our realm's innate light. May its essence gift you with the wisdom to know what is right, the strength to stay the course, and the love to act for the greatest good of all." Illuminara pressed her thumb to my forehead, drawing a small circle above my brows. A faintly sweet aroma filled my nostrils, and I drew a calming breath as my crown was lifted from its perch. We were almost done.

"This crown, dwarven made and crafted from the same piece of metal as the mighty Thor's, Mjölnir, channels the highest wisdom of our realm's great rulers. May its spirit imbue within you the gifts of insight, knowledge, and a clear mind in even the most difficult of moments." Illuminara slowly lowered the crown onto my head. Its weight felt heftier than it had a few minutes ago. I shifted slightly beneath the pressure.

"This scepter, gifted by Frigga and infused with energy from Asgard's core, channels the clarity of our cosmos' collective light." Illuminara lifted a long silver wand from the altar. It held a massive white diamond in its prongs, and as she held it over her head it sent rainbows dancing along the walls of the chapel. "May it guide you through the days ahead, acting as a beacon in even the darkest of times."

I held out one hand, and Illuminara placed the scepter in it. My wrist buckled beneath its weight, and

I quickly shifted so I held it in both palms. When the officiant gave a slight nod, I rose slowly to my feet, rotated the scepter so it rested in my right palm, and turned to face the congregation.

So many eyes . . .

"Will you solemnly swear," Illuminara said from behind me, "to uphold the virtues of Alfheim? To put her needs before your own, and to protect her greatest good at all costs? Will you act in her best interest, govern with wisdom and benevolence, and respect the natural laws that call all beings to shine within the collective light?"

I spoke in a clear, loud voice. "I solemnly swear so to do."

Illuminara stepped forward, to stand beside me. "It is my great honor to bestow upon you the title Queen Aura of Alfheim, Leader of the Light Realm and Bearer of Truth. Long may you reign!"

"Long live the Queen," chorused the hundred guests in front of me.

When I lifted my scepter, a fanfare of horns echoed through the chapel. I glanced at Illuminara, whose nod confirmed it was time to leave. Careful not to trip over my skirt or drop my crown, I descended from the altar with a stiff spine. As I passed Viggo, his dimple deepened—his grin absolutely radiated pride. I shot him a saucy wink before lifting my chin and continuing regally down the aisle. Once I'd cleared the back doors, I slipped into the waiting room, leaned back against the wall, and closed my eyes.

Thank gods that's over.

"You did it." I jumped at the deep voice coming from the doorway. It had only been half a minute—not nearly enough time for anyone to make it out of the chapel.

Or so I thought.

"My gods, Viggo. You scared me!"

"Apologies, Your Majesty." Viggo bowed at the waist. "I just wanted to be the first to congratulate you."

"Get up," I hissed. "Don't make this weird."

"Permission to approach the monarch?" His eyes sparkled.

"I said stop it!"

Viggo crossed the room. With his broad shoulders and confident stride, he was *definitely* owning the Prince Charming vibe. When he reached me, he dropped to one knee, took my free hand in his, and kissed my fingertips. "My queen."

"I swear to gods, Viggo, if you keep this up I will club you over the head with Asgard's Scepter of Light."

"You wouldn't dare." He tilted his face upward, giving me a view of his impish grin.

"I would," I threatened. "So get. Up. Now."

"As you wish. Your Grace." My boyfriend stood, and I lifted my scepter.

"Viggo Sorenssön, I swear, I am this close to—"

Viggo silenced my threat with a kiss. He pressed his lips to mine, sending a pulse of heat that shot straight to my heart. I wound my arms around his neck, careful not to drop the priceless Asgardian artifact I still carried in my right hand. With my left, I wound my fingers through the strands of his hair, curling the dark waves around one finger. Viggo slipped his hands around my waist and pulled me closer, pressing his hips against mine as he pinned me between his body and the wall. A groan escaped my lips, and I pulled Viggo closer, not wanting anything to separate us. We were partners in every way that mattered. And we'd conquered a hell of a lot of odds to get to this point. We'd made it through the academy and recovering the *Opprør* senators; we'd defeated Dragen and Rankin; and we'd come out the other side of both graduation and coronation days. We'd faced more challenges in the last two years than I'd hoped to in a lifetime.

We deserved a few seconds of celebrating.

But seconds stretched to minutes, and before I knew it, an impatient rap on the door pulled me from my kiss coma.

"Your Majesty! There are a *lot* of revelers waiting on you!"

Eunice's prim voice was the ultimate buzz kill. With a sigh, I gently pushed a disheveled Viggo away.

"Oh, wow. If I look half as bad as you, I'm in no condition to greet anyone," I said.

Viggo chuckled. "I'll stall Eunice while you put yourself back together."

He raked his fingers through his hair, restoring his waves to their former glory. Then he smoothed the front of his jacket, straightened his sash, and unlocked the door. "Hey, Eunice. Enjoy the ceremony?"

While Viggo kept my protocol advisor busy, I snuck over to the mirror in the corner. There was no recovering my hairdo, so I fluffed it with my fingers and decided 'beachy waves' would have to be queenly enough for this coronation party. I straightened my dress, adjusted my crown, and met Viggo at the door.

"You ready, *Glitre?*" he asked.

"As I'll ever be." I slipped my hand into his, and pulled him through the doorway, past a frowning Eunice. "Come on, Sorenssön. It's time to party."

CHAPTER 19

THE FESTIVITIES LASTED WELL into the night. After a formal dinner, we retreated to the ballroom for toasts, speeches, and finally, dancing. A small orchestra was set up in a corner, and they played waltzes, foxtrots, and other old-timey tunes that kept the visiting monarchs on the dance floor for the better part of an hour. When they retired to their rooms, the conductor picked up the tempo, drawing some of the younger crowd out with more upbeat music. But it wasn't until the orchestra packed up their instruments and the DJ Jande had commissioned took over that things really got good. Having been robbed of his opportunity to dance at last year's Solstice Ball, my fun-loving friend had personally selected the playlist for the second half of the evening. And Jande had made sure that *everyone* would have a good time.

An hour into his set, the DJ announced the party was moving to the garden. The palace had been prepped for an indoor/outdoor flow, so when we shimmied our way into the courtyard, strings of lights illuminated the roses and the lavender maze, and more were strung between the ivy arches. Combined with the full moon, there was plenty of illumination to what quickly became a dance-off. Maja and Rafe valiantly defended their title as ballroom champions, and Elin whipped out some Midgardian dance moves from before our time. Nobody knew quite what to do with her running man or funky chicken, and by the time she electric slide-ed her way out of the circle, Finna and Wynter were left scratching their heads.

"We used to do that in junior high to make each other laugh," I shouted to them.

"Are all the humans' dances that strange?" Finna asked.

"Some are even weirder," I said. "You should see the floss."

"They clean their teeth while they dance?" Finna scrunched up her nose. "Ew."

A bubble of laughter escaped my throat as Viggo pulled me into the circle. We danced for what felt like forever, taking periodic breaks to refuel on the trays of food the telepaths transferred from the ballroom to the garden. We'd had a seated meal after the coronation, but the party food was much more fun. I threw down one of everything, from sliders to twice-baked pota-toes, to brownies, to the tiny cups of ice cream from my favorite Granite Ridge malt shop that I'd described in great detail to the royal chef—and begged him to replicate for my big night. I was equal parts stuffed and exhausted when the DJ took a break. I had no idea what time it was, but when Viggo and I slipped away from the festivities and walked around to the front of the royal residence, the sky was pinked with the first rays of dawn.

"Race you to the waterfall?" Viggo shot me a grin.

"First of all, I'm too exhausted to walk, much less race. Second, I'm pretty sure I'm too full of ice cream to lift myself off the ground. And third, Rankin soured my taste for waterfalls, thank you very much."

"Not *that* waterfall—the one on the other side of the meadow. *Our* waterfall. The one where we had our first . . . you know."

Heat crept up my neck at the memory of the first time Viggo and I had locked lips. It felt like a lifetime ago that I'd discovered that Viggo and I were both faeries . . . and mates, at that. Had it really been less than two years?

"Loser has to wipe down the equipment in the palace gym." Viggo leapt in the air. He hovered a few feet away from me, flapping slowly so he bobbed up and down in front of one of the enormous pines that bordered this edge of the castle.

"We don't have to clean our own equipment anymore," I reminded him. "We have staff for that."

"Look who got all fancy." Viggo flew backward in a lazy circle. His silver wings accentuated the pale blue of his suit, and I couldn't help but stare at the way his shoulders flexed beneath the fabric. *Yum.* "I guess if you don't mind getting your butt handed to you by your future king . . ."

"*Way* in the future," I reminded him. "Like, *years* and *years* from now."

Viggo's dimple popped. "I can wait. Now get airborne already, and race me to our spot."

"Fine." I checked to make sure my crown was secure before bending my knees and spreading my wings. In one swift movement I was off, darting around Viggo and cutting in front of him so he spiraled to his left. He spluttered in surprise before righting himself and lowering his head. He adjusted his trajectory and took off again, following me around the pines and into a grove of conifers. "What's the matter? Too tired from dancing to keep up?"

"Oh, it's on." Viggo's laughter spurred me forward. We flitted through the trees, past the meadow, and around the backside of the mountain that led to our waterfall. As we crested the peak, I drew my arms to my sides and dove. I had just enough of a lead that I reached the grass first, tucking my feet into my chest and touching down in a *perfekt* landing. When Viggo hit the grass, I turned to him and placed my hands on my hips.

"Guess you're cleaning the palace gym," I said smugly.

"I thought we had staff for that."

I adjusted my crown, and my breath caught at the beauty of our surroundings. We'd landed beneath the massive willow tree at the edge of the crystal blue lake.

The mountain stretched above us, lined with moss and rocks and every conceivable type of flower—from the ones I'd known back in Granite Ridge, to blooms so exotic I'd never have pictured them in my wildest imaginings. Water spilled over the mountain into the pool below, frothing in a pristine white foam with a gentle mist hovering above it. I drew a deep breath, inhaling the sweet aroma of honeysuckle—no doubt coming from the patch situated just behind the willow. Everything about this spot was calm, and serene, and absolutely *perfekt*. No wonder I'd been relaxed enough to let Viggo take me in his arms and—

"Your Majesty?" Viggo's voice danced with amusement. "Where'd you go?"

"Uh . . ." Heat flooded my cheeks. "Can you repeat the question?"

Viggo chuckled. "Do we or do we not have a cleaning staff in the palace gym?"

"We do," I confirmed. "But I just decided they needed a day off. In honor of my coronation."

"Is that so?" Viggo stepped closer, until we stood just inches apart.

"Mm-hmm." I nodded. "And I like a nice early workout so be sure to have the weapons shining by six a.m. tomorrow morning."

Viggo snaked his arms around my waist. "Are you always going to be this much trouble?"

"Probably," I said honestly. "Is that going to be a problem?"

"Probably." He brushed his lips against my hairline.

"But I'll learn to manage."

"Ha. Ha."

I pushed against his chest, but he didn't move. Instead, he released his hold on my waist and wrapped his hands around my wrists. He brought his mouth to my ear, and murmured softly, "Just promise me one thing."

I shivered. "What's that?"

"Promise that you'll always be the stubborn, brilliant, infuriating, determined, scrappy, creative, beautiful creature I fell in love with."

I turned so my lips brushed against the stubble on his jaw. "Who are you calling scrappy?"

Viggo reached up to cup my cheek in one hand. He cradled my face, pressing gently until his lips met mine. His eyes blazed emerald fire as he slipped his other hand down my back and said, "I love you, *Glitre*." Then he claimed my mouth in a kiss that left my heart thundering, my head spinning, and every nerve ending in my body pinging with happiness.

Once upon a time, I'd been fated to rule a failing realm. And while now I had no idea what the future would hold, I knew I could face any challenge head-on with the support of my awesome friends, my trusted team, and the guy who'd had my back from the moment we became training partners. Viggo and I had a lifetime of adventures to look forward to. And no matter what the Fates threw at us, I knew we'd lead Alfheim to her brightest possible future.

Together.

ACKNOWLEDGEMENTS

As always, I owe all the gratitude to my adventurous family—I am so grateful that God gave me you! Thanks to my longtime editor, Lauren Clarke of CREATING ink. *Takk* to Mariana and Alison, for endless patience, thoughtful feedback, and the epic superpower of keeping this Viking ship afloat. Thanks to my beta readers, Laura and Lorna. And to the readers who took a chance on this little faerie tale—thank you for sharing your imaginations and your hearts with me. I couldn't do this without you!

And *tusen takk* to MorMorMa. Always.

ABOUT THE AUTHOR

Before finding domestic bliss in suburbia, internationally bestselling author S.T. Bende lived in Manhattan Beach (became overly fond of Peet's Coffee) and Europe...where she became overly fond of McVitie's cookies. Her love of Scandinavian culture and a very patient Norwegian teacher inspired her YA Norse fantasy books. And her love of a galaxy far, far away inspired her to write children's books for Star Wars. She hopes her characters make you smile, and she dreams of skiing on Jotunheim and Hoth.

Learn more about the world of S.T. Bende at
www.stbende.com.

Erik held me until my shoulders stopped shaking—whether it was a minute or an hour, I couldn't tell. The only things I knew for sure were:

1. *I was trapped a thousand years in the past, with little hope of ever going home. And,*
2. *I was wrapped in the arms of the most absurdly gorgeous Viking to have ever walked the face of the Earth.*

Maybe my old life was overrated.

When seventeen-year-old Saga Skånstad discovers an antique dagger, she's instantly sucked into a world where Vikings rule the seas and dragons roam the skies, and the only thing more dangerous than the chief who takes her captive is the rival who steals her away. The heir of Norway's most feared tribe is fierce, cold, and absolutely unyielding. With intruders encroaching upon his borders, Erik Halvarsson has little patience for the girl whose ignorance threatens his very existence. He enlists Saga in the magical Valkyris Academy, where she learns the skills she'll need to protect herself from foreign raiders and domestic terrors. But nothing can protect her from falling for the one guy in all the world she's absolutely forbidden to choose . . . or from risking everything to unlock the secrets that haunt him.

When darkness threatens Saga's new home, she must decide whether to return to the life she's always known, or fight for a love she never could have imagined. Her decision will determine a legacy—not only for Saga, but for the world she never knew she was fated to lead.

So nothing surprises her more than catching the eye of Tyr Fredriksen at her first college party. The imposing Swede is arrogantly charming, stubbornly overprotective, and runs hot-and-cold in ways that defy reason… until Mia learns that she's fallen for the Norse God of War; an immortal battle deity hiding on Midgard (Earth) to protect a valuable Asgardian treasure from a feral enemy. With a price on his head, Tyr brings more than a little excitement to Mia's rigidly controlled life. Choosing Tyr may be the biggest distraction—or the greatest adventure—she's ever had.

Learn more about the world of S.T. Bende at www.stbende.com.